# Once Bitten

**Order of the Dragon, Volume 1**

Tina Glasneck

Published by Tina Glasneck, 2017.

# ONCE BITTEN

**Death by accident, vampire by design**

This was supposed to be the cruise that would reignite the spark in my floundering romance writing career. My life changed with an awful splash into the North Sea. When hypothermia set in, I never expected rescue in the shape of Nessie – yep that Nessie, a dragon. He saved me, but, boy, what a cost.

The human me would have loved to live in a Scottish castle, in the Highlands no less, but something dark lurks here. This place is full of magic, other supernatural beings that are loyal to Alistair Campbell, the tall, gorgeous dragon shifter.

But, now someone is after me. Girls are appearing strangled and drained leaving behind vampire markings. My housemates are giving me the side-eye, like I'd break the cardinal rule in this world: don't reveal yourself to humans.

And now someone is trying to make sure that I'm wiped out.

Walking undead or not, if I'm going down again, I'm taking this wretched corner of the supernatural world with me.

# Chapter 1

**LESLIE**

*"It will be the beginning of the end, when the hybrid takes shape. Able to walk in the light, thirsts for blood, and walks among the gods without being one of them. Wielder of magic, seer, possessor of all. In darkness's death, would come forth a shining light—able to table the monster, not only as its mate, but its chosen bride."—Dreki Edda, Provision XVIII*

I DON'T KNOW HOW I'D gotten here. I stared out into the expanse of empty wilderness—rugged Scottish mountains with large trees, babbling creeks, and talkative wildlife waited for me to near.

Away from the winding roads and life of Inverness, my hand gripped the sword's grip and I tried to breathe. Even under the cover of night, with only a sliver of the moon casting its light, I could make out in the inky shadows the maleficence that wished me harm.

It wasn't an assumption, but one I could feel.

Magic shifted through the Highland air like freshly sifted flour.

The faint smell of freshly shed blood caused my hackles to rise. My canine's descended, a thirst beckoned me.

That aroma was like what fresh baked bread used to mean to me. I breathed through my mouth cutting off the aroma's appeal. The tanginess that was surely a trap.

With my sword raised, I inched toward the darkness, watching for the slightest movement.

Life was different than how things played out in fiction. My heart reacted to the tension, pulled tighter than a guitar string ready to be plucked.

But this isn't what I'd always been, a creature now of the night.

Vampire or not, this battle was one I'd have to fight.

*1 MONTH AGO, NEW YORK City*

"Are you breaking up with me?" I whispered.

Sitting across from my literary agent, I couldn't help the feeling of dread that began to climb up my legs into my hands until they tingled. Not like a heart attack, or even a stroke, but more like my life was soon to flash before my eyes.

My thick manuscript of 500 pages still sat on his desk, in the copy store's logo-marked brown box—not a page read or touched.

It had taken me years to find an agent. I'd created a manuscript I loved, pitched at writers' conferences, sessions, and cold-queried. Let's not forget the contests, ranging from stalking agents on social media for a chance to even thrust a few chapters to one in an elevator, or under the bathroom stall door.

Desperation. It stank to high heaven, even I knew that, but if I failed at this dream, I'd have nothing to land on.

"You really need to think about your career," Maurice Abernathy leaned back in his leather chair behind his overly large and neat desk. No manuscripts piled high, not a speck of dust to cloud that polished shine. Instead, he steepled his fingers and ogled me. "Vampires are some of the oldest of legends, and here you go trying to improve on something that people don't want changed. We know they have super strength and speed, but what is it that you think they should have but don't?"

"Magic?" I croaked.

"With magic, you need a magical system. It doesn't just appear out of nowhere."

I'd been method writing for years—learning all that it took to make my Viking characters come to life. Let's not even mention the rituals. I bit back my tears that threatened. I could feel it in the air. Change was coming and this one wasn't going to be good.

"It's not as bad as it seems, but the publishing house doesn't want to renew your contract."

"But time traveling Vikings are hot right now," I said.

"No, the market's cooled. I tried to warn you that readers just weren't grabbing the Viking things as much as the Scots. You wouldn't heed my advice." He leaned forward, and for a moment I saw the pity that drifted across them... but then again, maybe I just saw what I reflected.

"What am I supposed to do now? I have this conference you booked me o— this Woo Cruise."

The Woo Cruise was an annual cruise where romance authors, readers, photographers and cover models mingled for seven days and six nights along the British Isles and Iceland. There would be sessions on writing, as well as more pitching and of course, alcohol with half-naked models to bring the cover art to life.

"I've already paid for that out of my planned advance. You promised me—"

"I misspoke. I took Jim out for lunch and he assured me that the House was truly considering your potential, but the stats are the stats. You haven't moved out of the— no top rankings, no awards since your debut novel. Maybe you've just lost some of that passion. Some of the *reason* why you're writing."

Writing served as my personal therapy. I just shared it with the world. It healed my pain, but right now, I was at rock bottom. Without something coming in soon to change things, this dream would pop, and my livelihood would be gone way before anyone could even request a sequel. Yet instead of asking my questions, I remained mum. The words whipped around in my mind, creating a toxic and fearsome cocktail of desperation and the bitter taste of fear.

Maurice was already getting his fifteen percent from my efforts. He had all the contacts, and all I had to do was write. At least that's what he'd promised me what felt like years ago, but it had only been three years. Enough time for him to let me drop.

Instead of comforting words, he buzzed his assistant. "Molly here will see you out, and make sure you make it home okay, but on your way out, don't forget to take a package of my business cards to share with your author friends. When do you plan on picking up Stacy for the departure?"

"Stacy?" I sputtered.

"Don't you remember? You asked for an assistant."

I pulled back my shoulders. "Well, if I need an assistant it will *not* be from here. I might be downtrodden, and have to make it through these next seven days, but I will do it without your help."

"I understand. It is never easy to have to start over."

"But will I really be starting over? I am—"

"Writing is often like wearing a placard while naked, and asking people to tell you how you look," Maurice began. "In this sense, unfortunately you were found lacking." Molly entered the room. "Please see Ms. Cutlass out." He'd kindly reminded me of my government name, instead of the penname I'd been using, Leslie Love.

"Leslie," Molly said. "please, come with me."

I tried to pull my shoulders back, and to keep tears from streaming down my face in humiliation.

When I'd signed a contract to become a published author with Maurice's firm, here in prestigious New York City, I thought I'd made it. Isn't that what every author wanted? On kitten heels, I silently followed Molly out of the office. Away from the Fifth Avenue décor, away from the scented air that tasted like fresh oxygen being pumped into the rooms; away from the crystal vases, and original Tiffany glass. The overly plush carpet that practically swallowed my steps, and the floor to ceiling glass that partitioned the office space, all things that I'd helped to pay for on my mid-list earnings.

"Don't worry, Leslie. You'll bounce back. Maurice can be a jerk sometimes, but he didn't mean it like that. Go, enjoy your cruise, and refill your creative well—find that story your heart needs to tell." She signaled the elevator for me and waited until it arrived.

"Plus, who doesn't love cruises?" The elevator pinged, and I entered into its steel tomb.

"Me," I croaked. "I get sea sick."

# Chapter 2

**ALISTAIR**

Alistair MacLeod, upward from the breeze, waited for the buck to pause. His ancient navy and green kilt fluttered slightly. He kissed the bone-made good luck's piece, Odin's Amulet, which hung around his neck.

"May his spirit be received into your hands," he prayed, and cast his eyes towards heaven, and then tucked and the amulet back under his shirt.

All was silent. He could hear the beast's heartbeat, smell its sweat, and sense its warmth. He licked his lips, readied his arrow, pulled back the bowstring, inhaled a cleansing and calming breath, and took aim.

A loud ruckus from the forest's underbrush pulled at his attention. He watched the buck's ears perk up, as a swinish snort grew louder, coming his way. The buck then bolted for Gillianbusti, Alistair's trusty black wild boar who then loudly snorted and nudged Alistair further away from his hiding spot.

"What did you do that for?" Alistair asked. They'd been out in the rain and wind waiting for a buck to come their way, and now that it did, those hours lost were not to be recaptured.

"Yeah, well, you're saving its life isn't going to distract from the fact that we need something to eat."

Gillianbusti snorted again.

"Yes, I know that isn't true, but what else am I supposed to do? The Bifrost bridge isn't working, and that means I get to stay here in the Highlands until either the bridge is repaired or—well, I'd rather not think of the other options. The dragons have to be able to make it back to Asgard sometime, and not just stay put here on earth."

The large black boar double snorted.

"That's not an answer."

Over the centuries of them being together, they'd taken to creating their own way of communicating. A snort wasn't just a snort, but it presented with it a chance to communicate that otherwise wasn't possible, a code even. Gillianbusti wasn't a shifter, a god, or even a magical creature. No, he was simply dwarf-made, created in the forges by great dwarves, the sons of Ivaldi, which gifted the gods with all of their grandest of tools, and gifted to him by his great uncle Frey.

"Yes, I know, Oma Freyja was to send word, but she'd been quite quiet. Time in Asgard doesn't run like it does here. She and Odin are probably still trying to gain peace or whatever one does all day in Asgard. As long as I am not forced to visit the Dragon Queen, and stay off of her radar, well, we'll be fine."

"Snort."

"No, they are not taking pity on me," Alistair said, and packed his bow back in place. Just like those bowstrings, he was wired too tightly.

The responding high-pitched snort sounded like a guffaw.

As they were about to make their way back to the castle's keep, a sprig of wheat sprouted before them, and therefrom an envelope took shape.

"Mail from Asgard." He muttered and picked it up. Yet, instead of the usual parchment, when he opened it, a hologram took form and there he saw his grandmother, Freyja, standing. Her golden hair fluttering around her as a slight wind blew. She probably planned it that way for aesthetic.

"Dearest grandson," she began with a smile. "There is much you must know, but Odin has decreed, that you remain in Midgard, in the Highlands until such a time as boredom is the least of your worries. As the head of the guard, your expertise in making sure the gate is not penetrated is more important than your extended vacation here in Asgard."

"What, he wants me to sow some wild oats? Those days are over. What can mankind give me that I don't already have? And what of the door, well, nothing ever happens here."

"This is not a one-way telegram. I can hear you," Freyja said, and furrowed her brow. "You see, your playboy ways have gotten you in enough trouble over the years, all of those broken hearts and all, but Odin thinks you must learn that of love, honor and valor."

Alistair rolled his eyes. "Love is so... human."

"To be a god to humans, you must also understand them."

"My responsibility is to the Order. You get too involved in their lives. I live here off-grid, as they say, with the occasional dalliance. My home is a beacon for the supernatural and I rule this providence with an iron fist. There have been no reports of any supernatural avoiding the treaty, and thereby we remain secret."

"That is very good, you have been able to guard the gate to help keep Midgard safe. However, you are to head away from the castle some, as there is one that requires the Order's protection."

Alistair frowned. Occasionally, his grandmother found it in her meddling ways to suggest that he leave the castle grounds to go out in search of a supernatural being. Usually he could find a way to get out of it.

"You want me to deal with the living?" His words littered with disgust, as they usually didn't adjust to their ways. He'd tried it once.

And still regretted it.

Freyja nodded. "Even more. I want you to find the völva."

He felt his stomach rumble, his thoughts of hunting forgotten. For years, they'd been looking for the supposed Norse seer.

""I'd truly rather not have to deal with that right now. You see—"

""You don't have a choice."

"Why do I think the bridge is fine and this was more of your doing than that bastard husband of yours? If you can send me this message, surely you can also locate the prophesied one."

"You know he can hear you too. And your profaning his name will not make it all better, even if you do follow it up with a blessed kiss on your amulet. Your reproach is uncalled for. Do you really wish to rile Odin up in hopes of getting him so upset that he calls you to appear before him?"

"I've been in the Highlands since the whole Jacobite debacle. Trying to stay out of the way of those shenanigans almost cost me my head."

"Treason? Really?"

"People get suspicious when the lord of a castle never ages, leaves or does anything else normal. How many times was I charged with being a warlock? How many times was I told that if I didn't comply there would be hell to pay?"

"Really, dear grandson, I don't want to hear your complaints. You are really braver than all of this. Where is that alpha-heroism that the Highlands are known for?"

"I can kill someone without a problem. Slice and dice with the best, but do I really want to?"

"We're not commanding that you go to war."

"No, what you are commanding is that I find this woman, and that is like going to war, now isn't it? Next thing you know I will have to worry about the color of the curtains and putting something on under this kilt, not even to think about if I want to take vacation."

"You're doing it again."

"What?"

"Whining. No, that will not do." She clapped her hands and he caught a whiff of magic on the horizon. "It will appear now that guests shall be arriving, those who have been looking for you. You need friendship too."

He ignored her words. "Then since you know so much, why don't you come down here and find the lass to befriend—and while you're taking orders, can you make sure that she—"

"This is not fast food."

"You are telling me that I must seek out the völva, and we know what happens then, for her to live under this roof, she must become my mate, and I have no need. You just want to play matchmaker, like always. What I want is to be left alone, free from this place and an inherited duty that I did not request."

"Do what is asked of you. There is a ship nearby. Why don't you go have a look?" Freyja said. "And that is an order."

Alistair bent his knee. "Yes, my queen." The goddess's order he could not deny.

"I don't deal nicely with regular people. They tend to bore me, and let's be honest, I've yet to make the acquaintance of one that does anything more than stare. After living so long, I'd like someone to talk to, truly communicate with and not just an empty vessel—and such does not exist. If I wanted that I would have taken the genie's lamp offered to me in the Near East."

"Dearest Alistair, you talk too much. You don't take time to listen."

"Maybe you simply have nothing of importance to say."

"They have that Kobe beef you've been wanting to try, that you can't get there."

"When does the ship leave?"

"See, all you needed was motivation."

With a simple flicker of light the transmission ended and he still stood there with his boar, staring at his quandary.

He'd been alone for a long time, except those in his possession, the McLeod's near Loch Ness. They'd taken care of his castle, and he'd let them remain on this side of eternity instead of making their way to their final destination. It was the Viking way of things that he sought to disrupt. No pyre, no relinquishing of the soul to the afterlife. He had the powers of peace and an abundance of pleasure. What good was war in all of that?

Besides, what good was a woman if she only brought with her more war?

A LOUD KNOCK SOUNDED on the thick oak door, which echoed throughout the hall. The noise traveled to the library where Alistair sat waist deep in books.

"You summoned me?" Killian asked. Killian stalked in like the alpha he was, but his pack was comprised of other supernaturals—that was the strange way of the castle. The supernaturals lived harmoniously together, all working alongside one another to guard the gate from the pending attack by those who'd wish ill upon Midgard.

"Welcome back, dear brother, I trust that your trip abroad was fruitful?"

"I was able to see how the other half lives."

"Have a care; they are indeed a part of the Order. When did you return?"

"Well, I did the job well enough, as they have agreed to the treaty, but it is expected that the next Wielder is not set to arrive at the academy until next year."

The Wielders, or those who could invoke the magic of the gods, were rare, like unicorns, four-leaf clovers, and honest women.

"That is at least some consolation." Alistair closed his book. "Of course that is not enough. The time is almost upon us, as the prophecy has determined."

"Well, we're trapped until we find a solution. If we are able to bring the chosen into the Order, then we will be able to protect the gods."

"The only problem is that a woman hasn't crossed this threshold with any of those qualities."

"At least none that have fulfilled the list, but the research is surely enough fun on its own," Killian said.

"You might be finding Asgard between silken thighs, but if we don't find her, well, it will be the end."

"I take it that you have a plan?"

"All of those feelers are out. If the gods wish for serendipity to fall into my lap, I shall not be one to complain."

"Be careful what you ask for, dear brother, as the gods enjoy their mischief."

Alistair leaned back in his chair, "And I the chase."

# Chapter 3

**LESLIE**

What started off as a bad day could only turn out better, I hoped, and attempted to shake it all off as I popped my old suitcase open. Dust sprinkled the air from disuse.

"What is it Myrtle?" I called out.

"Oh, you must be having a bad day if I'm Myrtle and not called Gran," she chastised. She floated over to my side, as ghosts do, and leaned against the wall without falling through it.

"Are you going to go to the different ports, maybe even bathe in the North Sea?"

"No, and catch a chill? The water in July averages fifty-five degrees. I'm not looking forward to hypothermia." I placed in a stack of items I thought I'd need, and then turned to grab another sweater.

"It's a cruise, dear," Myrtle said. "With all of your research about the Highlands, and the Vikings, I'm surprised you haven't planned a special day trip on land." Gran pulled back her black lace veil, which completed her depression era morning ensemble. Her bobbed black hair framed her heart-shaped face and ruby red lips. She tugged at her black gloves as if they were beginning to slip down, and plopped down into a seat. "Oh my, woe is me," she groaned and placed her hand across her face as she leaned back in the chair and gave a loud sigh. "Who is going to take care of the apartment once you're gone?"

"You are such a ham," I snickered. "Mom had seven children. If I'm not here, one of the boys can stop by the apartment."

"The apartment that must stay in the family," she quipped and I watched her peek out from beneath her arm. "And I know my dear daughter birthed a little bit more than half of a football team, but you are special."

"You can open your eyes now." I crossed my arms, as if I were the mother and she the child. "If I didn't have to go, then I wouldn't."

"I can feel it from the ether. Something bad will happen if you go. Do you have all of your vials with you?"

I shook my head. "That was all research."

"You dug up black henbane for the gods' sake. You can't tell me that was research."

"I also burned a little of it, and dreamt of dragons, so we know that is all."

"The gods were trying to give you a sign," Gran urged. Of course, since she was a ghost and I wasn't, it wasn't like I could argue about what the gods had in store for me or what happened after that final breath on this side.

"No, dragons don't exist. Magic doesn't exist, and the supernatural world that I'm aware of is only in my fiction—present company excluded. The dragon had to be from something I was watching. That's it. Let's just change the topic."

Gran wagged her petite finger, the one that held one of the largest baubles I'd ever seen. It's true though, what you're buried in is what you haunt in too. "You don't have to get testy about it. The ritual was still a ritual, and it opened you up. I've been telling you for a long time that you are a seer."

"Just because I see you, doesn't make me anything special. There are more important things to deal with than this supernatural mumbo jumbo, like this cruise. If I don't go, we won't be able to live in this subsidized apartment in the middle of Manhattan—a deluxe luxury that no one understands how I'm able to afford."

I pinched the bridge of my nose and tried not to scream. When Gran got it into her head that something should be done, nothing less than an exorcism was going to get her to change her mind.

"You should cast the runes. They will agree with me." My great grandmother had a way of being overdramatic.

And it wasn't because she was dead, a ghost, and I could still see her.

I wiped away the imaginary sweat on my brow. "Gran."

"Stop. I hate when you call me that." She fingered her black pearls.

"Okay, Myrtle."

"Enunciate it dear. It's like that beautiful beach. You're butchering my name today." She pushed herself out of the chair, fluffed her flapper hair, and retrieved a cigarette out of thin air. I wasn't sure how she still held on to her cigarette holder, and all of the charms from then, but things had a way of appearing—like she had an invisible ghostly vault.

"Well, if you go, then I am going too." A nice trunk materialized and she sat down delicately on it.

"You can't just leave this place."

"I can with this." She held out her hand and therein rested a lovely gold and onyx Art Deco mourning ring. "Check in the back of the safe and you will find it there. Your mother was always one to break tradition."

When chaos ensued, that meant that Gran always had a plan. I could almost swear that her need to make sure her family was okay was why she refused to cross over. She'd been a young mother, and watched everyone grow up under this roof, and participated as much as she could.

Of course, it helped that the females of the family had an opened third eye and could see her. As a kid, it made for interesting play dates.

I opened the safe and reached in the back. And just like she said, a ring was indeed there. I pulled it out and paused. Gorgeous didn't begin to describe it. A deep purple amethyst rested in its center, surrounded by seeded pearls and diamonds. It bore the inscription: *Myrtle Davidson who died June 28th, age 23.*

"You should really stay here."

"Nonsense, and miss the chance to see the old country that my mother always told me about? She'd left behind poverty and persecution for hope of a better life here. She just didn't know—

"She'd have to head to Ellis Island to find her happy ever after." I finished in unison. "You know that was the basis for my first novel."

"Yes, if you throw in a shifter or two."

"If I'd tried to tell the story that my grandmother, twice removed, ran away from Scotland because of a dragon, I would have been laughed out of Maurice's office."

"Sure, but you also would have told the story of your heart. You've been laughed out of there now, haven't you, dear? And you are no closer to being happy with what you write. Story comes from passion—like delicious food. Our history is so rich, reaching all the way back to King James Court. Now that is a story you must tell—that of the trumpeter's daughter."

I shook my head. Ever since I could remember, Gran had been telling me stories of dragons, and royalty, and how her family had received precious gifts from the king himself.

"I tell you, Scotland is magical."

"Well, I don't plan on really making land. It's a cruise around the British Isles and up to Iceland. All I can hope for is that I don't freeze." With this in mind, I plopped another sweater into my suitcase, and clicked it closed.

"No matter. Put the ring on, and then let's go. A grand adventure awaits us, and surely, you aren't going to leave me here to be ignored by the others?"

"The others being my brothers who can't see you?"

"The others also being those henpecking spinsters who refuse to walk in the light. I told you that old Mrs. Goldstein still refuses to leave until her great-grandson fulfills his promise—a promise of a five-year-old has little meaning, I told her, but she won't listen. No. She remains, haunting that apartment until he becomes the next pop star. As if scaring the poor child to make him practice his music isn't futile."

"Didn't you try that on Dad?"

"Yes, but that was to shut him up. He sounded worse than a cat in heat. And according to your mother, she'd made sure he'd been fixed." Her eyes crinkled. "See dear, some things are meant to be."

I could only smirk. Gran wanted an adventure and I wanted a paycheck. Plus, what harm could there be in taking an extra passenger with me?

"Before we go, let's try the henbane again. I think it will clear your vision," Gran said.

"You're just trying to kill me. Too much of that stuff is deadly. The next thing I know, you're going to suggest that I drink mistletoe tea, and yes, that's toxic too."

"Well, love, I do have a fondness of death. But if you die, how will we ever take the cruise together?"

I rolled my eyes. I eased the ring onto my left middle finger. It was a perfect fit.

"Come, let us begin before I have to get to the port." Gran clapped her hands in glee. "Might as well turn the chanting music on to get an authentic experience."

"This is going to be the best thing. You won't regret it!"

# Chapter 4

**ALISTAIR**

Alistair pulled on a dry dress shirt over his wet body. For the past five days, he'd been jumping aboard cruise ships in hopes of allowing the magic to lead him to the seer.

"Blimey, nothing," he swore, and buttoned up his shirt.

But the queen's orders were to be followed, as she was over the Order of the Dragon—the top spot—and everyone had to defer to her judgment, even him being the leader of the Scottish branch.

Loud classical music echoed in the chamber, where only a torch's light shone. He moved to the chamber's center and in the soft dirt with his dragon claw, instead of his human hand, he leaned down and created the holy sigil.

And therein sprouted a Valkyrie before him. Kara, one of Odin's strongest female warriors. Her silver armor reflected the tiniest of lights, and her raven black hair cascaded over her shoulders. A thin golden tiara rested on her head with Odin's insignia engraved on it. "I'm sorry, dear Alistair, but her lordship cannot be reached now. She asked if it is urgent that I come in her stead."

"I've yet to find the seer," Alistair huffed.

"Do you, oh mighty dragon, seek help in doing as ordered?" He could hear the contempt in her words.

Instead of answering, he cast her a charming smile. "Surely love, you have more that you can help me with than just words."

"The last time I helped you, I ended up in the equivalent of a time out. You were considered a distraction."

"And still when I call, you answer."

Her frown faltered.

"We can never be together, Al, and your charm will not do anything but cause me to remove my sword from its sheath and see if your innards are more human or beast. I will not betray my king, or oath."

Alistair raised his hands. "I would never ask you to do such. Instead, I ask for your help, assistance that the King and Queen need not know about."

"I cannot wield magic any more than you," she said. "But there is a plant that can help you: bog myrtle."

"What the bezerkers use?"

"Yes, for you, it should allow you to see that which is not seen by the eye. Your blood has magic in it. You are not just a wielder of it."

"That is stating the obvious."

She reached into a pouch that hung from her belt, and passed it to him. "Don't say I've never done anything for you."

"And this will help me find the lass? So, I can then stop chasing cruise ships like a bloody dolphin?"

"I'd say more like a shark, but you get the picture." She chuckled. ""Got to love what the queen has you do."

Alistair palmed the bag.

"You will also need to ingest just a small amount," Kara said.

"What happens if I should ingest too much?"

"I've never seen one of your kind take this, so I can't say. I'm not a healer or herb witch."

He reached into the pouch, pulled out a good pinch and put it on his tongue.

"There's no tarragon in this, right?"

The herb danced on his tongue until his mouth numbed, and spread slowly through his body.

For the briefest of moments, the classical music that had been playing shifted, and he heard the chanting music. He closed his eyes and stood in an apartment from the looks of it. Outside her window, he heard loud vehicular noises, as her window was slightly ajar. A woman with unruly, reddish curly hair sat on a sigil, palms up; her words melting with the ancient chant of Kvasir, the god of poetry. Her face he could not see, but the comforting scent of lavender enveloped him. "*Mine.*" The beast within him roared. A sound he was not only unfamiliar with, but also didn't quite recognize. In all of his years, that had never happened.

He further scrutinized the apartment, until his gaze fell upon a stack of luggage nearby, and on top of that, a cruise ship ticket.

"*Eureka!*" He practically screamed.

Just as soon as a vision of the woman's face began to appear, she disappeared again.

Alistair opened his eyes.

"Well, at least that's a start," he said and nodded his head. Now he knew exactly who he was looking for and where to find her.

# Chapter 5

**LESLIE**

When I'd agreed a cruise to Scotland would be great to re-spark my career, I'd somehow forgotten that whole seasick thing. Instead of dancing in the dancehall, eating any buffet, or even playing shuffleboard, I'd succumbed to bouts of unease. With each sway of the ship, my stomach flip-flopped and thought to lurch.

Although Gran decided to travel with me, she seemed to have taken an interest in all of the other people on the ship. I'd never heard her rousing chuckle reverberate so loudly through the halls.

Twilight, with the sky painted in beautiful blues and purple, the sun waved goodbye, and music played from the live band on the deck above.

I leaned over the rail of the cruise ship, watching the waves slap against its side. The salty sea air did nothing to ease my plight. My stomach lurched, and I thought I swallowed a bit of my vomit.

"Don't keep me waiting," Claudine said with a slight giggle. She wiggled her fingers in a slight ta-ta, and practically lost a hip, pushing it to the side to accentuate her curvy figure.

"Did you hear that?" Claudine said moving to my side. "He's going to take me dancing."

I tried to smile at that. She'd been trying to set up a meet-cute with Donovan for months, and I'd given her the greatest of excuses—a themed cruise with authors, readers, and photographers with their cover models.

Donovan looked great in leather. He looked great in cotton. And from his covers, he even looked amazing in Scottish kilts. I'd booked him often enough to grace my book covers to know all of his smoldering looks, even his bedroom eyed gaze. And I'd seen him work his magic on an assistant or two.

Claudine was not my assistant, just my best friend.

I wiped my mouth with a hanky, and pushed away from the ship's rail.

"You do know that he's a romance cover model?"

"Yes," she sighed.

"You do know that he's surely meeting a lot of women on this trip?"

"What is that supposed to mean? As long as he likes a little sport afterwards, that's fine."

"It might just all be a game."

"Well," she stuck out her ample chest, and pulled her halter top higher, as if gearing up for the challenge. "I'll just have to play for keeps. You might know about fictional love, but I know about men."

"As long as you don't leave this one tied to my bed in my room, we'll be fine."

"Leslie, it's all just for research. How are you ever going to describe a real adventure without living it?"

“That doesn’t mean my jumping on the popular trend of whips, chains and ball gags.”

“Don’t forget the anal beads.”

I wrinkled my nose. But that’s Claudine, always thinking about ass.

# Chapter 6

**ALISTAIR**

"You called for me?" Lloyd trudged forward. His graying hair thinning, and his back a little hunched. Blue overalls sloppily rested on him, and his too-big-for-him Wellies thudded against the floor with every step.

"Yes, dear man. How goes everything down at the farm? We haven't had time to catch up as to the caretaking of the property."

Lloyd had been with him for years, way before the old man began to hunch over. He'd known Lloyd from his youth, and watched him grow older, and hopefully wiser.

"Things are okay, sir. This year's harvest is set to occur on time."

"Harvest?"

"Yes, the cattle have to be culled."

Alistair grimaced. That was not what he wanted to discuss this morning. Culling wasn't the thing he wished to be reminded of. Life was confounded and complicated by death.

"And the tenants?" Alistair asked. "Are they well cared for?"

"As well as tenants can be. Of course, you need to invest some monies to patch up those cottages that border the property, as well as the fencing." Alistair stared at Lloyd. In all of his years, he'd been an honest steward, yet the more they conversed, the more he questioned.

"Didn't we just invest a few thousand pounds to repair them?"

"Yes, sir, but the most recent storm came through and caused a good amount of destruction. If you'd like, I can take you to see them tomorrow—"

"No, no, I completely understand how difficult it must be to have to show the progress to me by night. Instead, we shall come up with a plan."

"A plan, sir?"

"Yes, it will be helpful to make sure that everything is tended to in a timely and efficient manner."

Lloyd stared down at the floor. "Sir, I've served your family for a good number of years, as did my family before me, and we've never done anything that might cause your lordship harm."

"You mustn't fret." A mischievous smile crossed his face. "But see, I can feel when things are a little off, and since you are speaking about money, I can only believe it has to do with that, or is it something else?"

Lloyd gulped. "It is something else, my lord. I was in the village today, and I heard the whispers again."

"Whispers?"

"They say that the beast was seen again, swimming in the loch. The beast that not only eats our sheep whole, but has also kills our women."

Alistair frowned.

"And there is evidence that this beast is responsible?"

"Yes sir, it eats the sheep whole and then spits out the bones, leaving them for us to discover. It happens once a month and concurs with the sightings."

Alistair knew that Killian, during his raids, steered clear of populated places, and stayed on the protected and sacred grounds. Folklore had a way of ever expanding around these parts.

"Do you think we have something to fear?" Alistair stood from his chair, placed his hands behind his back and began to pace.

"My father once told me about the beast, who we've called Nessie, and how he once saw it too—looked him in the eye and thought to eat him too, but he was able to fight it off with his paddle. What if this Nessie has returned and is again trying to eat the villagers? Could that explain what is happening to these women too?"

Alistair's mouth went dry. There was much the world didn't know, and much he still questioned, but even he couldn't determine what was true and what was just make-believe, folklore.

"Come by tomorrow, Lloyd, and I will have a check ready for you," he said and nodded his head, dismissing the older man.

Was he the monster doing all the damage and causing calamity?

He shuddered to think that this beast of what he must become was the same one killing. This meant, he'd have to reach out to Freyja again. Why would she require him to take part in such horrible acts? But he didn't remember a thing of such attacks.

"I have a proposition. I think we can catch it, but I'm going to need a little more money to get all of the people to agree and join in on the hunt. It will take a lot to catch Nessie."

Alistair frowned. "I'm sorry. I thought we were talking about the tenants and the land, not hunting Nessie."

"Aye sir, but that is why the tourist come here. If we can catch Nessie, then we could save our sheep, and imagine the fame the area would get—all of the tourists."

Alistair could almost imagine it. Lloyd had been seeking one scheme or another since they'd met, and even after working as the castle's caretaker all of these years, he was still looking for a quick way out.

"Are you not happy here, Lloyd?"

"Of course, sir. This job gives me almost everything I want."

"Almost?"

"Well, I do think there is more you could be doing to get along with the town's folk. Throwing open the doors and allowing them a gander around might help."

Alistair sighed. Every couple of fortnights passed until the next conversation came up about money; Nessie or the town's people. But he couldn't blame Lloyd, as the runes still guarded him from seeing the truth throughout the castle. Instead, it appeared just like any other historical structure. He didn't need to see the ghosts or other supernaturals walking around.

"But Nessie's been swimming these waters since the 500s. We should capitalize on that and draw in the tourists. That could mean a new world for the town."

Alistair tried to find a way to let the old man down gently, but so far, he'd unable to do so "We're a little sleepy town and like it that way. Plus, if we catch Nessie, then it will drive all of the other towns on and near the Loch out of business too. Remember, we have to think about our kin."

# Chapter 7

**LESLIE**

"You have to get over your sea sickness," Claudine said.

I shook my head as if I agreed, but to be honest, there were worse things in life than not being able to take two steps without getting nauseous. I kept my food down, but at a price. I stayed hanging over the rail. That was better than remembering the strangeness from the sigil.

*I could've sworn someone was there.*

"Today is all about you performing." It was her way of telling me that the cruise was about work, me hustling to remain a brand name even after flopping with the latest release and contract.

"What's on my plate for this afternoon? I asked.

"Well, you have the author meet and greet on Deck C, with the other romance authors from the Fleur group.

"Why was I signed up for that? I don't write French books, nor are my books translated into French."

The cruise had been booked prior to my knowing that the anvil was going to fall. If this had been an Acme movie, there would be tons of gags to pull, but this was life.

"No worries. Surely, you'll have enough to talk about and even some rabid fans. Did you send out your newsletter inviting your readers?"

I scratched my head and wondered why I had an assistant.

"That's what you were supposed to be doing," I mumbled.

"Well, too late now. You might want to stop grabbing on to that metal pole as if it were going to save your life. This sea breeze isn't helping either. You have to go and engage with your readers."

I felt like a fraud, letting go of my comfortable nausea for a discomforting smile. Imagine having spent years creating something to have it all go "poof" overnight, and then to have to declare it still a success the very next morning.

My walk from the deck to C deck was filled with gloom and doom, or at least what I wanted to equate it too. The ship rocked, passengers bypassed me, and with each step, my hands began to sweat, my stomach flip-flopped and beads of sweat dripped down my brow. My mouth parched, I attempted to swallow to create some saliva to relieve what felt like the sands of the Sahara Desert.

Upon arriving to the venue, I noticed the three tables set up—and two of them had lively banners, with cover models showing off their detailed six-packs and hardly any face, colorful table clothes, and amazing swag all set up. Yet, on my table rested a simple white name shield—and my name was misspelled.

"You know, in my day, people cared about their appearance," Gran began.

"Shh." I clenched my teeth, sighed and eased my brow. The tension in my shoulders sought to keep me from standing there tall and proud, because what I felt was almost overpowering.

"Ms. Love?" asked an attendant. She reached out and I shook her hand. "Thank you so much for coming. Your books are under your table. Since we were not able to get them to be returnable, any books that you don't sell, you will need to reimburse us the cost."

"But my publisher..."

"Yes, they stated that you would be fine with that." She then handed me a copy of the email exchange between her and Malcolm.

"I told you those people would rip you off." Gran whispered so only I could hear her.

I gritted my teeth and a laugh erupted. To my own ears it sounded harsh, uncomfortable even. It reminded me of the cutting-edge sound that a maid might make to the child who happened to order her about—unable to chastise him for fear of losing her job; it was the smile that resulted from stress, fear even; the smile that resulted from a quagmire's plight.

Here I stood, needing the money—could I even say that? I'd taken my last pittance, betting on a new contract, a new book deal, and a new bout of sales to send me erupting from the red to the black. I'd paid with blood, sweat, tears and my needs be damned. I'd poured my soul into words that many refused to read. Still, there I stood, and I knew she saw it too—the fraudulent writer who could not speak of success, but of mistakes, failures, and even more missteps.

"That should be fine. With all of these people here, I don't foresee any problems."

"Of course, don't forget we have the luncheon right after this, and then another signing time. You'll be seated at a table with readers who stated they enjoy your genre. Then you can engage them, build a relationship."

"I believe in getting to know my readers," I said. "It's not about if they buy something from me."

She nodded her head as if she understood, but I knew she didn't. For her, a business was based on if the company's bottom line produced revenue, not on if the company increased its social engagement.

"Readers are so much more than dollars and cents," I said.

"That might be the case, but don't forget the stipulations in the contract that you still have to fulfill." She let the rest hang. It seemed like my situation was indeed well-known. My contract for work may not have been renewed for an additional project, but it was still expected that I perform according to the contract I was under.

She turned away, and I noticed two other women walking forth with speaker ribbons on their name tags. They seemed to be deep in a pleasant conversation as their laugh reached my ears.

"Ladies," the attendant said. "I am so happy you could make it, especially with your schedules. I must say, you two are amazing, and I love your French heroes. Jean-Luc is so dreamy and Pasquale is just amazing. Maybe you two might collaborate on a future project," she gushed.

In that moment, extreme peace descended over me. That was why I wrote books. Not to be idolized, but for characters to become three-dimensional people that readers connected with, and the great thing about romance is that jealousy wasn't something that needed to exist. The pie was big enough for all of us. I moved forward in greeting.

"Hi, I'm Leslie Love. You must be Beverley Hyacinth Madeline and Florence Plusherson."

We smiled at each other and moved around the table.

"We're so excited to be here," Beverly began. "This is my first Woo-Cruise, and it's just so exciting. Don't you agree Florence?"

"It's like a girl's night out with tons of hot men for eye candy. So far, I've met so many wonderful readers, and did I mention the hot men?" she snickered.

"Don't say that too loud, or your husband back in Texas will hear you."

"What happens on the Woo-Cruise stays on the Woo-Cruise," she said. "Besides, there is nothing wrong with a lot of looking, and he gave me tons of one dollar bills."

"I don't think we're supposed to be making it rain like at a strip club," I said.

"Oh no, that's not what I do with them," Florence said. "I give myself a dollar for every time I don't give into temptation. I hate to see money left on the table, even my own. But there is this one model here that is fierce. He did a lot of those vampire and shifter covers. Mesmerizing eyes; muscles that are so hard and throbbing." She began to fan herself. "Such kissable lips."

"Florence," Beverly said. "I'm not sure Jim's going to be happy with you all hot and bothered about this."

"Jim?" I asked.

"Her husband and my brother. She's my sister-in-law."

Florence began to fan herself with her nameplate.

I took a step back. I could feel my eyes widen. If she was getting hot and bothered by talking about a handsome man, what was this woman about to do when the cover models showed up in the next couple of minutes?

"Well, they *are* just playing parts. We don't invite strange men back to our bunks," Beverly chastised.

"But what if I really, really want to? I mean, I love your brother and all, but my imagination is satisfying me more than he is. I swear, he's cheating on me with his damn secretary—yeah, cliché, I know, but I can't find any other reason that he's lost interest in me. I started writing some erotica, right—something to get him to read—and he won't pick it up. I'll sit there for hours wearing my best lingerie, and he doesn't even notice. Something is definitely wrong, and I'm sort of sure it's not me."

"Florence, I didn't know."

"Well, there's a lot you don't know. So, if I choose to sit in a corner, drink my margarita and undress a handsome model with my eyes, it's because that's the closest I'm going to get to getting laid anytime soon."

Before Beverly could respond, a group of readers showed up and made a beeline for the two women, leaving me at my pretty empty table to stare at them.

Whoever this cover model was that she was interested in seemed to keep Florence hot and bothered.

Of course, as that thought popped into my head, Donovan also showed up.

# Chapter 8

**ALISTAIR**

Not too many people would notice him if he snuck on board, he surmised and at the nearest chance, he boarded the ship.

He aligned with the cruise ship and hopped on board. Then grabbing the stern of his boat, he lifted it from the water and folded it up until it fit nicely into his pocket. That was one of the many great things about having a magical ship, after all, and not wanting to get wet—appearing as a dragon might have been too frightful, that he knew all too well.

The cruise ship was alive with people. They were everywhere—and loud. Of course, seeing all of the banners with half-naked men made him question exactly what type of ship he was on. Some of the men were dressed as Highlanders, others as Vikings, and Arab Princes, and still others had on modern day suits with ties they liked to wiggle. Even more men walked around with fake axes they liked to swing, and swords they didn't know how to hold.

Of course, Freyja hadn't said which ship he was to sneak onto, and dog's bullocks, at least this one here came with an open bar and more food than he'd ever seen.

"Are you lost," asked a blonde dressed like a Viking Thrall.

"Is there something happening on this ship that I don't know?"

She leaned over and touched his arm. "Oh, you're so muscular. I just had to touch and see if it was real."

Alistair stepped back and straightened. "I don't like to be touched."

"Then how is it that you're a romance cover model. All of these women on this ship will be fawning over you."

"Uh...romance book covers?"

There was a reason he avoided humans. Some thought that he should be petted, felt up, and that the thought of their "come hither" glances were nothing more than repulsive to him. He wasn't asexual, he enjoyed a good romp. But some of these women were so hungry for male attention, he wished he'd sent Killian on this trip.

Killian would have found a way to lay every woman here flat on her back.

The lady shoved a book down the front of his pants and gave it a pat.

"Just want to make sure there is no false advertisement," she cooed.

"If you'll excuse me," he meandered through the crowd, and somehow or another discovered the pool area with half-dressed women and men dancing and splashing water, while bright lights flashed in the background, and loud music reverberated throughout the room "Party!" someone yelled and splashed into the pool beside him.

Alistair didn't know a lot about romance novels. He retrieved the one from his pants, and glanced at the passionate cover on the front of what appeared to be a Highlander romance with a lot of wind. The author's name, Leslie Love, was scrawled across the front in a fancy, soft pink calligraphic font.

"It's true. This is Helheim."

# Chapter 9

**LESLIE**

We'd made our stop at port, and I was happy to stay behind, but now, as the ship refilled, it wouldn't be too much longer before we left Inverness behind.

"There are some fine looking men here," Claudine said. She took a seat at my table and began to ogle the numerous male specimens that found their way in viewing distance. Her head turned, following the latest man who walked by wearing Chinos and deck shoes. She picked up her fruity drink, which I'd noticed she'd been sipping on all day.

I yawned, and took a sip of my water to wake up. It wasn't that I didn't appreciate the handsome specimen onboard, but cover models didn't usually do it for me. I liked manly men. Men that looked like they could hold their sword and do something with it.

"Yeah, but they're just not my type," I said.

"Is it because of that whole beige rage?"

I frowned. "I like men; strong men, with defined abs, sculptured shoulders, strong jaws." I began to fan myself. "He can be blue for all I care. He just has to know how to woo me."

“Girl, this is more of a booze cruise than a woo cruise. If you wanted that, we should have taken a single's cruise.”

I smirked. The last time we'd done that, she'd left with an STD, and I with my credit card overdrawn, planning that the next royalty check would pay it all off. Nope.

“If you want to know the truth, all I want to do is try to relax some, clear my mind and let all of that bullshit go.”

“You and me both.” Claudine turned at the latest man crossing the threshold into author central, and sighed. He must not have tickled her fancy. “I'm going down to the pool.”

“I thought you were devouring all the lobster you could eat.”

“Trust me, I'm having some delivered to the room every night I'm here. Yum.”

“Don't forget they have a nice spa area too,” I called after Claudine. She threw me a wave and headed towards the beautiful blue pool. Her pink flip-flops thunked against the deck paneling, and as I stirred my lemon-ice water, I felt a pair of eyes staring at me.

Turning, I saw a beautiful man who made me pause mid-stir. My hair fell forward over my sunglasses, covering my eyes.

Now, I'd seen pretty men before; I'd seen extremely handsome men before, but this one—he put them all to shame. Tall, ”six feet two, distinguished, as though he wore the outfit and not the other way around. His ink-black hair hung in long luscious waves, and his beard; neatly trimmed, covered a mouth that quirked at my gaze.

My mouth went dry.

“May I help you, Miss?” His accent was filled with a Londonesque ease, and his eyes as inviting as cool silk on a summer day. He was decadent. I licked my lips. I hated to blink. I could drown in that gaze. A strange feeling lapped in the pit of my belly, churning.

"Um, I was just trying to get my thoughts straight," I said.

He smiled a Trident commercial smile.

"Can I help?"

*Charming? Check.*

Before I could agree, we were interrupted by the model I'd been avoiding.

"There you are," Donovan said.

I shuddered hearing his voice. He'd somehow gotten fixated on me and wouldn't leave me alone.

"One moment," I said and turned away from Mr. Walk-out-of-my-dreams.

"I've been looking for you," Donovan continued.

"Sorry, I was here talking to —" I turned around and the mystery man was gone. Had I imagined him? Had he been there and just vanished?

"Who were you talking to?" Donovan asked.

I swiveled my head searching for the handsome man, but he'd disappeared like a soft caress.

"Guess I've been in the sun too long."

"Well, if you don't hurry, you'll be late for the next thing on your schedule." He proceeded to pull out a piece of paper that had my itinerary on it.

Alcohol stank on his breath. This Donovan was different than the usually cordial and professional model that understood the constraints of publishing. Without my series continuing, he wouldn't be gracing any more of my covers.

"Why do you have that?" The ship was too small to have my personal stalker on it right now.

He quickly folded it and placed the paper back in his pants pocket.

"I'm not going to let my piece of golden honey get away from me. You know, your cocoa butter scent drives me wild." He slithered closer towards me.

I took an unconscious step back and frowned at him.

Ever since I'd discovered his picture at some convention and begged my publisher to put him on my covers, well, he's been sickeningly sweet. Sort of like the stripper that has no interest in you, just the large stack of folded ones in your pocket.

I placed my hand up. "Whoa. Although you might consider that a compliment, it isn't."

"Does my adoration offend you?"

"I find your behavior very offensive. I think you're drunk."

He shook his head, and clenched his jaw. I could see the muscle working.

"You should really get to that workshop you need to lead." He cleared his throat, and I didn't know him well enough to have any idea what might have been happening behind that handsome mask, but whatever it was, the evil glint in his eyes gave me pause.

"I'm sorry. I didn't mean to offend you," he continued, then turned and stalked away.

Gran materialized at my side. "You need to be careful with that one there. He's been poking sheep so long, he doesn't know that you're a wolf."

"Wolves hunt in packs. If I were anything, I'd be a vampire."

I grabbed my glass of water, glanced at the clock, and headed toward conference room A.

"You always did have a thing for those that sucked. I was just hoping you'd have better taste in men than your mother."

# Chapter 10

**ALISTAIR**

What in all that should be holy is going on? Thoughts swirled. He moved from the pool area, and towards where the authors seemed to be convening.

It didn't take long before he noticed her.

He watched as one model seemed to do a body roll, while another author stuffed dollar bills somewhere. He couldn't be a prude. There was one author that sat to the side. She had a name tag on with a folded piece of paper before her. She looked as miserable as he felt.

But it was the scent of lavender that made him recognize her.

He'd seen beauty, he'd tasted it, rolled in it and practically drowned in it, but it wasn't her. She was different. A spark flunked and made him stand still.

That didn't happen too often, had never happened to be honest.

There was something in her aura that caught his attention. The more he stared, the more his stomach did something strange inside. His palms grew sweaty, and for a man that always had something to say, he found himself speechless.

"*Mine!*" He heard something within him call out. His eyes blared and he stared at her, taking in every nuance of her heart-shaped face, her curly reddish-brown hair, and kiss-worthy lips. He wanted her to smile and be the reason a smile crossed his face.

He couldn't make words form, couldn't move. A gust of wind blew, rocking the boat. He needed to get his emotions in check, or he'd sink the whole damn ship.

He wished for nothing else than to push his chest out, remove everyone from around them, toss her over his shoulder and take her away—far away from those who did not deserve her attention.

She was breathtaking. He paused and frowned. Rubbing his chest, he realized that he didn't like that quite much.

She'd only be a distraction in the castle. To him, the Order and everything that he'd created over the years—that was what mattered.

"Oh, do you read romance?" An older woman who reminded him of his grandmother; white hair and wide rimmed spectacles, said as she pulled on his sleeve. "I've seen it all, but I didn't think that men like you would read such things."

He cleared his throat. "Men like me?"

"Yes, manly men." she emphasized manly and touched his arm a little longer.

"I'm a great fan of Ms. Love's work." He held up the copy of the book that had been shoved down his pants.

"She's all right, but she'll never be as great as Cassidy MacFarlane. She writes authentic love stories, not this crap—" She waved at the woman whose name he'd read off of the paper placard.

"You, my dear, just don't know good story telling," he said

"I prefer the stories filled with BDSM. That is true smut. Just my taste to get the engines going and you know, revved up for someone like you to finish me off."

Alistair tried to keep a straight face. Of course, he probably hadn't had sex since before the woman standing next to him was born, which made for an uncomfortable conversation. "You know, sunny," she continued, "men like you need to know the rules of foreplay. It's not all about poking and prodding, but you got to make *love* to a woman. Those MacFarlane books can teach you how."

She shimmied her hips around in a circle. When did great-grandmas get so sexual?

"Um?" He looked for a way out. He'd been alive when women showing a bit of ankle was cause for scandal, but this? This lewdness he couldn't handle. He could feel the walls closing in when the woman began with the talks of whips and chains.

"You know, when I was younger, I made sure to use what I had, and that's why I'm still able to keep going. Helps to keep me young."

"Not sure your husband would agree with that," he said.

"He was too busy with the housekeeper. I kept the pool boy." She turned and swished away, leaving him to consider her statements. It had been a long time since he'd had to consider wooing a woman, and he just wasn't ready for that. The potential.

His thoughts shifted to the last time, and his ex. Skadi. They'd been hot and heavy and then when things became difficult, she became difficult.

She taught him that love wasn't worth it, but maybe Ms. Love could teach him something else.

On that thought, he turned away not liking where those thoughts could lead.

The seer would only cause problems, and even his allegiance to Freyja wasn't going to make him take that *woman* back to his castle; this was now simply out of the question.

# Chapter 11

**LESLIE**

The ship rocked and careened as the waves continued to crash against the sides. My dinner gown swirled around me from the ship's breeze, just as my head swam from the constant movement.

At the starboard side of the ship, I held on to the deck railing. Music from the Top 40s blared, people laughed, but where I stood, no one was around, not even the waiter who'd been plying me with drinks.

The star-filled sky offered me a moment of relief. They twinkled, and so far away from city lights, and land, I appreciated the different constellations.

The boards creaked behind me when someone appeared.

"My dear, are you okay?" Donovan asked.

I turned to see the cover model that'd been on the list of Claudine's "to do" tonight.

"You look quite dashing in your finery," I said ogling him in his Scottish regalia.

"I've also worn it as it has historically been depicted." He winked at me. That should have told me something was off.

"Is this about the next book?" I asked.

"Good, I'm happy that you're bringing it up, for it appears that the publisher has told me that you will no longer require me on your books." He came closer. "Don't you think I am handsome enough to cover your hard work?" His voice lowered to an intimate whisper. He pinned me against the railing, his arms on either side of me. His breath spiked with the odor of alcohol, warmed on my face.

I stared at him and wondered at his beautiful face. He was handsome in his own right, and if I would have had a thing for men in kilts, he'd have been right up there, but something in me cried out. I wanted a bad boy—a historical bad boy bezerker, and everyone knew that they only came as Vikings, even if later on those Vikings became some delicious Scots.

I cleared my throat, but unable to move. Instead, I batted my eyelashes. "You know, it's an interesting thing with the Scots and their tartans. Each one represents a clan. Which clan are you supposed to be from?"

"Surely, the only thing that matters is whether or not this Scot's sword shall pierce you."

"Pierce me?" I laughed. "Did you just say pierce me? I know you are trying to play a part, but that is not something to joke about. A historical man wouldn't talk like that."

He furrowed his brow. "Are you laughing at me?"

I turned away and watched him clench his fingers around the metal railing.

"I'm not the first, nor will I be the last."

He leaned in, as if to place a kiss on me. I pushed against his chest. "No"," I said.

"You know you want it. I've read how you've talked about my body being on yours and how you've desired nothing more since seeing me."

"You are just the model."

"I am the man behind the muse." he took his hand and reached below as if to pull up the hem of my dress.

"No," I said again, and pushed at his chest.

"Isn't this just like you want it? Rough."

Closing my hand, I jammed my fist into his face. I didn't have five brothers for nothing. "I said, *NO*!"

"My face," he yelped, and grabbed his nose.

He'd get less covers now for sure.

Anger marred his features just as much as his broken nose. "They'll be no blue ribbon below from me, dear lad. Why don't you go get some sleep? Evidently being around all of these women has gone to your head. Better yet, why don't you just go?" I pointed back toward the lounge area.

He slinked away, and in that moment, momentous relief rained down on me. I hadn't had to defend myself since the sixth grade, where I'd been called an epithet, and it didn't sit so well with me then. Just as attempted sexual assault made me want to beat the shit out of someone—Donovan in particular.

I turned back around and stared out at the sea in front of me, watching the dark water. The only light came from buoys in the near, and that was all right with me.

I closed my eyes and drifted to the thought of what it would be like if he had been like I'd always wished for—a Viking. Maybe then I would have been more interested in knowing if the railing could have held me up or not.

# Chapter 12

**LESLIE**

With one piercing scream, I flew over the side of the deck railing and plunged into the dark frigid waters. My dress tangled around my ankles and legs, pulling me down further and further from the surface as I attempted to propel myself upward. Its heaviness acted like weights.

Time wasn't on my side, I knew, for the longer I stayed in the water, the higher the chance that hypothermia would set in.

For a moment, I could hear uilleann pipes playing as I attempted to move. My lungs burned, fighting to breathe, while a thousand needles punctured me. My heart contracted, and hiccupped. For a moment, my mind drifted to the Titanic and all of those souls lost on that ship, and how Rose had enough room on that damned raft, but refused to scoot over for Jack to also survive. I wished I had a raft or a life vest.

Like giving birth, I finally broke through the water, and as in the movie, in the dead of night, only stars lit up the sky. In the distance, I saw the ship's lights moving further away.

"What are you doing out here?" Gran said appearing at my side. Her eyes were wider than saucers. Her mouth formed into a large "O".

"I fell overboard," I sputtered.

"Fell or thrown? I told you that model wasn't any good."

My teeth began to chatter, but I couldn't really think. My head ached. "I'm not ready to die, Gran."

"And die you shan't. Stay here, and I'll go get help."

I'm not really sure where she expected me to go, but the more the waves moved back and forth, the more I longed for a life vest, some buoyance.

A numbness crept upward from my fingers and toes, and no matter how much I tried to remain calm, anxiety peeled me like an onion, ripping away layers at a time. My muscles grew tired.

And the waves pulled me under, again.

The battle was on.

I screamed as loud as I could. "Help me!" Yet in the inky darkness of the water no one could see me, and I couldn't see anything as the lights from the ship faded from my sight.

My eyes welled with tears, and as the waves rocked me back and forth, I thought about poor Jack. He'd frozen holding on, and I wasn't sure how long I could keep treading water before the sea would also suck me under. Large almond shaped blue eyes stared back at me.

Titanic had been my favorite movie up until now. I'd cherished the love story, and often fell asleep with the soothing sound track. But the more I tread water and thought about it, the angrier I became.

"Jack didn't have to die, just like I don't have to."

We were miles off of the coast, I knew, but the sea isn't like the ocean. The current would push me southward. But again, the more I behaved like a fish, the higher the chance I had of becoming shark food. I gulped. And a fresh shiver of angst raced through me.

"Help is on its way, dear. I made contact," Gran said, appearing again at my side.

"Whatever you do, don't you leave me again. There are things in this water that can devour me in one bite, and I'm getting tired. I'm not sure how much longer I can keep this up."

"Don't you worry, now. I'm not going to let anything happen to you." Her voice shifted, and she began to chant—something I'd never heard her do. Her voice filled a void within me, and I closed my eyes and continued to tread water, repeating the tune she sang.

Suddenly, a beast rose out of the water. The starlight reflected off of its large scaly frame, and its head—the size of my mother's minivan—reared up.

"Dear, your help is here. Now climb on."

I heard what she said, and I stared at the beast before me. Its reptilian eyes took me in, and waited.

"It's a freaking dragon!"

"Get on, dear, before you catch more than a chill. He will bring us back to the coast and get you right back on your cruise ship. You'll see."

It moved closer to me. "He?" I whispered.

"Yes. You mustn't be afraid. Not everything is as it appears. You should know that. He is here because he's magical and that's why he could see me. "

If she could have, she would have pushed me onto the dragon's back, and I would have let her. Instead, I took the last bit of my energy and splashed over to the waiting beast.

He exhaled, and a large poof of steam floated upward when he lowered his head, then I climbed up on its large back. The dragon's scales shimmered slightly under my hands.

"Your Gran tells me, dear Lass, that you need help," the dragon said. It's voice in a rich, poetic Scottish accent.

I flinched away.

"Don't be afraid, dear," Gran said. "There's a reason you can hear him, but that can all be explained later."

I wrapped my hands around him, and held on tightly, as he took to the water.

# Chapter 13

**ALISTAIR**

The last thing he wanted was to sit down on a make-shift throne and watch his boar rut. The odd thing was getting more action than he was, with half the effort.

He flipped through the pages of the book again. So far, the story followed an Ivan Macleod, a Viking at that. He couldn't help his guffaw. Sure, this Ms. Love had done her research, but there was so much he could teach her about that time period.

"Can you two stop it! I have no desire to watch this spectacle," he yelled and tucked the book in-between his cushion and the throne's frame.

"It is what happens during mating seasons, your lordship," said Benson Abbot, his manservant.

The castle overflowed with activity and was situated overlooking a Loch; his nearest neighbor lived twenty minutes away. But it was the way that the night lights played and danced in the sky that made his home a respite—one that they could not so easily get rid of.

With a bustle of movement, in hurried Killian. "Another letter has arrived from the township regarding the castle. They say that you are not following the rules in making this into a national treasure."

"Bollocks. They are no more interested in my registering this estate than they are in whether or not Nessie indeed exists." He smirked at that. Nessie had been seen too many times in the area to be considered local lore or even a folktale.

"They are just trying to search the caves," Killian said. "You know this problem is going to snowball. It's going to bring with it more of those ghastly Nessie hunters."

"The caves that they don't have access to due to the wards?"

"Correct. The power of the gods, elven magic, and all of that have kept us safe." Killian leaned back in his chair, stretching his arms behind him.

"I was surprised you took that trip to the ship?"

"Freyja likes to instigate things, and since I owed her a favor or two, I promised I'd make an appearance. Who even knew what an author cruise was"?" He shrugged.

"Didn't you see anything or anyone you might fancy?"

"Fancy? You surely jest? You're starting to sound like Freyja."

Freyja was his grandmother, and although married to Odin, and the Queen of Asgard, she still liked to play matchmaker, even with her grandson who had no need for love, or a mate.

"Why is it that you put on that dragon skin then, if you have no need for such triviality as mankind's interest?"

"Simple, my man. Boredom. Have you not seen the reactions of- mankind when the dragons arise? I mean, people come out here for a good show, and I expect to show them just that."

"Surely, that is what Gillianbusti expected for you to enjoy too—a good show."

Gillianbusti, the dwarf turned boar had become his friend over the centuries. They had made the best of an odd situation. Gillianbusti liked to entertain, he'd give him that.

"And I should just let him have his fun?"

"At least let him finish. The poor thing doesn't get to let loose, right?"

Alistair crinkled his nose, and frowned. He removed his shoe and threw it at the rutting boars. "No, I think I'd rather not have to watch swine engage in coitus. The noise is unbearable, and he might be my mate, but that doesn't mean I have to watch."

"Surely, you jest. He is cursed to be your companion, and until you are able to reverse the curse, he will remain punished in this here shape. What would you have him do?"

"Why not go in search of truffles"?" Alistair couldn't get them to stop, no matter what he threw at the pair.

"It's the middle of the night," Killian asked.

"It will give him more to do, and as you remind me, he is bored of keeping my company."

Killian nodded, rose from his seat, and shooed the boars apart, cautious of their thick tusks.

Alistair cared not that Gillianbusti didn't get a chance to finish. Like him, he should also be celibate waiting for his proper mate and not go chasing after the first piece that walked his way. Of course, he couldn't help but worry as to whether the other boar was indeed on tomorrow's menu, and shook his head.

There was never a better time to go vegan than after one's pet had fiddled the food.

As Alistair sat there and concentrated on what he should then do, he saw the white wisp of a woman flutter by. Her screams of help loud enough to make the undead awaken, if they weren't already.

"Madam, madam," he called after her.

The old lady appearing ghost settled down before him.

"You can see me?" she asked.

"Even more, I can hear your horrible voice and cries. What is it that you want?"

"My granddaughter. She's been thrown overboard and will surely die if help does not come soon," she said. He'd never seen a ghost panic, and watched her practically shake in worry.

"What would you have me do?"

"Can't you send out a boat? She was thrown overboard. I have tried several different places, but this is the first place where I've gotten a response. If you don't, she'll die."

"Or be already dead."

"If you can't help, then don't waste my time," she said.

"Time, looks like your eternal time is already wasting."

He sounded like an ass, and he didn't understand why. The more he considered it the more he recognized it for what it was—he needed an outlet for tonight, and the guise of Nessie would be a great trick!

"Okay, I'll help you, but you must promise me something first."

"And what is that?"

"Your granddaughter. You must promise her to me."

The ghost nodded. "I will do anything to save her."

"Good, for I am a beast and need companionship."

# Chapter 14

**ALISTAIR**

"This way," the ghost said.

Alistair shook his head ignoring her pleas.

"I know these waters and will find her, if she is there."

Diving under those waves felt like flying. He and the water became one. Sure, he had a boat he could have taken to pick up the lass, but what fun would that be?

As a mighty water dragon, he moved in and out of the water, embracing the freedom that the water gave him. He no longer worried about the problems that would still be there when he returned. No, instead, all he focused on was his breath, and the way his muscles propelled him through the water.

Four feet high and twenty-five feet long, he measured larger than many of the boats on the waterway. Under the blanket of night, and deep in the water, he moved through the school of fish that darted out of his way, as well as the other animals: eels, sharks and fish. He could feel her in the water.

There was warmth and not the kind created by a tinkle, but of a heart calling out to him.

He shook his head. A deal was a deal, but that did not mean he needed to love her, just that he needed to possess her.

He moved forward and as the distance grew from his home to the woman in the water, he took in the sight of her—it was the woman from the cruise ship.

"I wouldn't be surprised if you did this, Oma," he cursed his grandmother, and still closed the distance between him and the woman that gave him pause.

She'd taken his breath away during their short exchange. Her eyes sparkled, and in that moment, he could have gifted her the most magical of things—unicorns even, but right now, it felt more like a betrayal.

She wrapped her arms around him, and he felt her arms, her heart, her thoughts. He knew everything about her in that one touch, and thoughts assaulted him of how things could be between them if given a chance—a promise of ecstasy, passion and unbridled love.

He'd have none of that.

He pulled away, but she held on strong, until she'd wrapped her body around his own.

Images played of what could be between them, a future not yet built, a future that was only a premonition. When he'd first laid eyes on her, he'd seen forever, but never knew that forever could start right there with them.

She muttered something, and her voice filled with a hint of desperation and hope.

"Shh, lass, you need to rest. You are safe with me." *As safe as safe can be*, he thought.

"I'm not safe with anyone," she said.

Her pain struck him.

"Worry not, you will be home soon."

"Home," she muttered upon his touching her with his rune covered scales; she morphed before his eyes, the magic of the sea and of the gods and embraced the power of air, giving her the ability to breathe underwater like a mermaid.

His mouth gaped open. In all the magic he'd used, he'd never seen such. She wasn't a mermaid, he knew. He was to make sure that she arrived unharmed to his house, but still, it freaked him out.

And not much could shake Alistair the brave.

*Gods don't freak out, they just create something else*, he considered. Well, that was his thought until he reached the dark caves.

Prophecies can't be forced into fulfillment, even for one as beautiful as her.

# Chapter 15

**ALISTAIR**

Alistair followed the doctor, Peter, the residential herbalist and mage, out of the room into the corridor, where the woman rested. Inside, her Gran, the ghost, stayed at her side. He couldn't allow the doctor to say it there, but he knew the truth too. She had a bluish tint, and even more, her heartrate was lessening.

"I gather that you didn't wish for me to say my opinion as to the state of things in the room," Peter said. "I am not a medical doctor, but all of the signs are there. She will not make it."

Alistair nodded his head. He didn't know a lot about humans, but he did know that hypothermia, when it set in, left little chance of survival. Although he'd rushed through the waters to get her there, to the safety and warmth of the castle, every delay worsened it. Soon, her spirit would leave, and there was nothing he could do about it.

The hallway door opened, and there, the shocked grandmother stood. For a ghost once put together, she now appeared disheveled. "Although you try to hide from me this truth," she began, "I know she is dying. There must be something that you can do."

Alistair shook his head. “Death is a part of life. Although you are still here, that should also not be so. We must all rest.”

Peter interrupted. “There is a way, but it is a risky and pricey one,” he began. “You might not be aware of the legend of a mighty dragon, but it is said during the reign of King Frederick of Thule, that one of his sons was saved by a dragon.”

“So, a dragon can save a mortal?” Gran asked. “If this is so, you must try.”

“But it comes with consequences.” Alistair waved his hands. He didn’t want to consider what it would mean to be tethered to her. “Everything does.”

“She won't last through the night,” Peter deadpanned.

But was it worth the risk? Could he let another woman die because of his failure to act? The seer, if she died, what did that mean for the prophecy, for him?

Again the beast rumbled in his chest. “*Mine.*”

“What is this consequence of which you speak?” Gran asked.

“She'll become undead,” Alistair answered. “A draugr.”

“A what?” Gran asked. Her eyes blared.

“She'll become the equivalent of a vampire, thirsting for human blood, and unable to die. She'll also be tied to me.” Alistair shook his head. He could deal with everything except that whole ‘tied to you’ bit. If he'd wanted a mate, he could have found one to fill his bed on a permanent basis. Rose, his ex, had been enough of a hassle when she’d attempted to wrap him around her finger. Sex and commitment were two different things. He didn't need either. They came with consequences, nightmares, and power-hungry women that sought to make him heel.

"We're running out of time, sir," Peter said. "What would you like to do?"

Whichever decision he made, there would be hell to pay.

# Chapter 16

**LESLIE**

Have you ever awoken and had a hankering to kill everyone in a room, and of course, desire to crack every skull within range? The room was filled with darkness, the curtains thrown open, and the moonlight shone brightly inside.

Rage filled me with a heat. It was a combination of thirst—like the morning jonesing for hot coffee, combined with a desire to peel the skin off of every living soul, yank out their hearts and drink from the tap.

"Leslie," I could hear Gran's voice through the cloud of rage, but it did nothing to calm me. The voice I recognized as my own growled. I struggled against binds around my wrists.

I wasn't into any kinky sort of stuff, and the loss of control riled me up more.

I screamed. The guttural sound ripped through the room, and when the door opened, faces I didn't know approached me. But I didn't care about that. Instead, my gaze raced toward their necks. I could hear the blood whooshing through their veins, their hearts thudding to push the sweet blood.

Even their sweat smelled appealing. My mouth watered with want. I struggled more against the ties and bared my teeth.

"If she keeps pulling like that, she's going to break free," said one.

Snap. One arm broke free.

Felt like heaven to be able to move.

I tore free from the other restraint and leapt from my four-poster bed to the female who stood only a few feet away. She smelled like fresh ginger bread. I inhaled deeply and leaned forward.

My canines descended, and I reared back my head.

There would be no consequence. Nothing but my hunger mattered, my appetite had to be sated.

Her neck was so close. All I had to do was lean in closer and allow my teeth to sink into her delectable flesh, and all of that warmth would fill me.

As I reached forward to bite down, strong hands gripped me and tore me away from her. I kicked and clawed. Only air shifted through my fingers. I wished only to bleed her out and bathe in the warmth of her fresh blood.

I snarled like an angry beast, only then to whimper in a strange plea.

"I want just a taste," I plead. My eyes filled with crimson tears, blinding me. "Just a taste!" I demanded, and pushed back against the strong arms holding me down.

A new wave of rage rushed through me. The anger spread, and in a heartbeat, I stared at the man I hated. *Him.* There was no shade of gray. Any attraction that might have been there, he'd poisoned.

"No, Leslie," his voice commanded me, and my limbs responded. I could no longer struggle. I no longer pushed against him. Instead, like a dog brought to heel, I stood still. At his word, I was to obey his every command. And every second I stood across from him, I heard hearts beating and cursed him for not allowing me to sate my hunger.

"This is for your own good, dear." With a snap of his fingers, I again sank into this black abyss of unconsciousness, with the putrid stench of fish burning my nose.

I really hated sea food.

I CRACKED MY EYES OPEN. I didn't know how long I'd been out, but the happy sigh from my Gran told me all I needed to know. She'd been afraid and I'd pulled through. Snuggled in thick blankets around me, a fire roaring in the large fireplace, I glanced around at my surroundings. I was in what appeared to be an ostentatious room with white wall paper, and carefully chosen furniture. I rested on a plush settee in the salon. Two sconces rested on either side of the large fireplace which roared to life. In the corner, a grand piano waited to be played.

Expensive taste. Designer taste, not on a budget for sure.

Oil paintings, of who I guessed must have been the dragon's keepers throughout the ages, hung on the walls. They all appeared in Edwardian, Regency, and Victorian aged dress in their portraits.

Surely later, I could take in the grand architecture and interior design that displayed a coat of arms, with a dragon, of course.

My body wasn't my own. It felt scratchy, cold even.

"What do you remember?" Gran asked.

"Dancing?"

"You don't dance. You've hated dancing since you discovered what it meant to not have rhythm." Gran took a seat on the side of the bed. "You had me worried, and I'm sure you remember more than what you're telling me."

"I had a bad feeling about this trip and I was telling you the truth."

"Yeah, lesson learned. I should always listen to my ghostly grandmother."

My thoughts drifted from being in the water to the dragon's arrival.

Riding the dragon hadn't been as easy as it sounded. It wasn't just a thing of holding on and hoping I wouldn't fall off its back. The air was frigid far above as we flew, and against the beast, its heat sought to warm me through.

Despite the large flame, I shivered, unable to get warm. Although, all my thoughts of Rose and Jack disappeared once I'd reached land again, my head still ached from treading water for so long. I felt strange.

Gran patted my hand, what she'd always done to soothe me. Interesting what you could do with a small gesture.

"Hypothermia had set in, right?" I asked. Questions rolled off of my tongue. "What's happening"?" I asked. "and who is our host? I can't be so rude as to not introduce myself." That always got my lips to moving.

"The dragon, dear. He saved you, and seeing this magic, I think it's going to come with a cost." She shook her head. "We'll have to see about that, but for now, you rest."

Concern marred her brow, and for a ghost, that was saying something. Usually, her face was serene as a Sunday dinner, but this was as concerned as a food-poisoned lunch. With her brow furrowed, her lips pursed, if she could have moved things, she would have.

She came closer. "I just need to pull this blanket up higher around you."

"We both know you can't," I said. Ghosts could do many things, but moving physical objects was not one of their abilities.

She reached forward to tuck in the thick fur blanket around me.

And it moved.

We stared at each other wide-eyed, and I stopped breathing for a moment.

Gran lifted her hands and stared at them.

"Well, there's only one way of knowing for sure." She headed towards the door and instead of walking through it as she usually would, she slammed right into it, and stumbled backwards.

That meant one of two things: either Gran could now do the ghostly impossible or I was dead.

When I thought about death, I never thought heaven would be in a Scottish medieval castle. Heaven? Geesh.

"Well, you can't just sit there and think there isn't work to be done," Gran said. Her mouth said one thing, but her eyes were as large as dinner plates.

A knock on the door startled me, and in entered a young woman with her hair pulled back into a tight bun. Her plump freckled face and bright smile should have calmed me down.

It didn't.

"What's going on?" I asked.

"His lordship just asked that I check and see if you needed anything. You were in the water quite a while," she said.

"We're fine," Gran responded. For those who didn't know her, it was a polite smile. For me, I knew that smile—she was calculating and thinking about everything that was going on. If this were a recipe, someone just added a pinch too much salt into her Bundt cake.

I stared at the room a little more. "He definitely has an affinity for boars."

"Boars?" Gran asked, raising a brow.

"They're everywhere."

"Does this bother you?"

"No, but what if we've found ourselves somewhere where they hunt people. I mean, hunting is something that everyone can do, but I don't have to like it." I rambled. Tears pricked my eyes. Death. Geesh. "How is it possible to be here? Where is here?"

# Chapter 17

**LESLIE**

I struggled to my feet, needing to see more of the place than just this room of mounted boar heads. It didn't matter which color his tartan was supposed to be, I drew the line at taxidermy.

"Keep the curtains closed," Gran warned.

I nodded not understanding. I was never one to throw back the curtains and announce, look at me. Instead, I liked privacy, but I also noticed again that there was no sun.

"Gran," I called. "Do you think we can sneak down and explore this place?"

Gran sat on the bed. Her body becoming corporeal and incorporeal within the blink of an eye.

"I can't seem to get this right," she muttered.

I'd not seen her so confused, so out of sorts.

"What do you think this means? Am I about to disappear? Can I die again?" Her voice rose and fell, and I felt her anguish.

"We just have to find out what this place is."

"I can tell you what it isn't," she muttered. "For me to be moving from the realm of the dead back to the living, well, we have problems."

"Maybe it's not you, maybe it's me." Who knew that the confession of death might be so soothing. "I mean, I was out in that water a long time. And so far, this place does remind me of all of those historical novels, mixed with a lot of the paranormal."

"Historical romance novels," Gran smiled, placed her hand to her brow, and called out, "Oh, woe is me. Oh, kind sir. It reminds me of those books you've been writing."

"Yeah, the books that the publisher kept saying aren't selling," I muttered.

"Well, at least that got you out of your funk." I think she must have considered what my death would have done. She'd been with me my whole life, and I was glad that she was with me now.

"We're together, and I'm not ready to leave you" I said, then reached out to hug her.

"I would hope not, so let's grab a candle or flashlight and see what we can discover."

"Curiosity killed the cat," I said.

"That doesn't matter if I'm already dead."

Gran shrugged and helped me pull out drawers until we found a flashlight. "This should do."

"I'm sure he has a security guard on staff," Gran whispered as I sneaked to the door and cracked it open, looking both ways down the hallway to make sure it was clear.

"Yes, but are they like mall cops or armed guards with swords and armor? Those I'd love to see."

"Yes, you always were after a man with a long sword." Gran snickered at her joke.

"Eww, those are not things I'd like to discuss with you."

We followed the corridor until we came to a landing with French doors.

"Why is that?"

"Because, you're like my mother in so many ways."

"Dear, your mother was always a nincompoop. She never was one who believed in magic and look." We slowly opened the door and followed the winding stairs down into a cool, dark, dungeon.

"I don't think this is a good idea," Gran whispered.

"Too late to stop now. I hear voices."

Once at the bottom of the steps, and from afar, I watched this large pointy stone glow in an unearthly bluish hue. Illuminated, it cast shadows onto the surrounding trees, and the closer we moved, the more I saw other ethereal beings being called toward it.

"What is this place?" Gran asked. Again, her face was balled up in fear.

"But it sort of calls me too, Gran. I can hear what sounds like one-thousand voices calling my name at once."

"I don't think you should go there."

"But I have to." My feet moved of their own accord closer and closer, and as I stretched my hand out to touch the stone, the voices united sounding much like a large choir, then chanted: *"Forever united, forever apart, until you become one of heart."*

"LESLIE," ALISTAIR CALLED. "What are you doing down here? Please come with me. I'm sure you and your gran are starving."

"Oh, I don't eat. I haven't been obsessed with food for almost a good one hundred years now. Why don't you two get to know each other, and then we can all chat."

Gran wanting me to get know some male? I wasn't sure how I was supposed to feel about that. At home, she used to just sit across from me and watch me eat. Nothing like having someone stare at you to curb your appetite.

I allowed Alistair to lead me back above.

"All of your questions will be answered shortly. I had the chef prepare your favorites."

The thought of food made me gag, and let's be honest, I enjoyed food like anyone else. My best memories came with a food memory. I couldn't recall what I did last week, but I could remember that I had the best Monte Cristo sandwich from Bennigan's in 1998.

Although I knew that all the different foods on the table should have been appealing, it was like attending a barbeque and finding out they only had veggie patties and imitation cheese—it might all be filling, but it sure wasn't going to be enjoyable.

"How do you know what they might be?" I asked, a tinge of fear lit up my words.

"Simple, we are connected. Right now, I could write a dossier on you and reveal all of your hidden talents." He flicked his tongue at that note.

"Whoa, cowboy. I don't know what my gran may have told you, but I'm not that kind of girl. I may write about sex, but I...

I don't just go jumping into bed with the first handsome man I see."

"You find me handsome?" Alistair flashed a bright smile. If he were a dog, this would've been akin to me rubbing him behind the ears, and his wagging his tail.

"I also find it strange that you're a dragon one moment, and then this god of a man standing before me, but I'm keen on waiting to hear the truth of the matter."

"Well," he moved behind me, and guided me towards the wonderful dining room table that had all of my favorite foods spread about—from Thai to Italian oven brick pizza, to authentic Philly cheesesteaks and Cheddar biscuits, even my gran's cornbread that was thick enough to look like cake.

"How...?"

"Magic." He pulled my high back chair and I eased into it, smooth as a butler. I didn't notice when he moved forward and poured me a glass of red Moscato.

"Not what I'm usually in to, but since you insist on this."

"What are you talking about?" he asked. "I've been to several vineyards, I've never had this."

"It tastes like a flat soft drink with a kick."

"I might as well have told him that it tasted like number 40 dye for he quirked up his left eyebrow and nodded as though he understood, and I knew he understood nothing.

"Is your goal to stuff me?" The words tumbled out of my mouth.

"According to what your gran keeps telling me, yes."

I spat out my drink across the white table cloth. I wanted to kick my gran. She loved for me to think about getting laid, and I sort of still hated him. Not sort of, I still did.

The food looked delicious, like 'food magazine preparation' delicious.

"I've never met anyone like you." I could feel him putting on the charm, and I wanted to smack him—and that was so unlike me. I wasn't a violent person, unless you count the body count in my fiction. I understood death, and right now, instead of being pulled into his charm and vigor, I just wanted to rip off his head, reach down his throat, and be free.

"I would say that was a compliment."

I noticed that we were alone. With a place so big, I'd expected it to be filled to the brim. There was space enough for all of those here to join us. I might not have seen them all since coming here, but I could certainly hear them.

"Where is everyone?" I asked. I could practically hear them all on the other side of the walls.

"What do you mean?" he asked.

It felt like he was belittling my observation skills. I gripped my fork and shoved the sweet potatoes from one side of the bone china plate to the other side.

"The ones who are in this castle? But they are not joining us for this fancy feast."

"They do not like to intrude when we have guests."

It was like having thin walls. With all of them so close, I could hear every shifting of material. My senses were on overdrive with the voices, every noise. My head started to swim.

"Are you okay?" he asked.

"This is quite silly," I said and held my head in my hands. "I am not feeling so well."

"That is to be expected in your condition."

"My condition?"

He shrugged. He was hiding something. An undercurrent of anger tinged with that of secrecy ran between them, and for a moment, I wasn't sure I wanted to remain in his presence one moment longer.

"You should speak with your gran. She can inform you of all of the things that have transpired since your fall from the ship."

"Secrets are never a good thing to have," I whispered.

"Some secrets are simply there because the truth is not to be told by the person being asked. Your grandmother can inform you of what has happened and the consequences thereof."

The tiny hairs on the back of my neck rose. His voice held a warning that I didn't understand.

He quickly pushed back from the table and stomped away like a prepubescent teen, just like my brother used to do after watching the Brady Bunch back in the day.

"Sheesh, what was that all about"?" I too rose to head back to my room. If I was to start asking questions, might as well start with the one person I trusted, Gran.

Everything appeared too perfect. The more I thought about it, the angrier I became. He seemed charming, but that was also a lie.

I should have been happy to be surrounded by every part of my research—what an author's dream—but everything around me was a lie. I could sense all of those mythological creatures around me, and even their magic.

He lied to me, and brought me here to strip me of what life meant.

This had cost me my freedom!

As the anger rose, my canines descended. I'd never be happy here.

# Chapter 18

**ALISTAIR**

Alistair gritted his teeth. He didn't often leave the safety of the castle, but tonight he didn't have a choice. He pulled the black wool coat around him, and tried to keep to the shadows. Instead of driving into the city, he traveled across the estate sticking to the tree line, crossing over the ancient cemetery, and winding through until he bounded out onto the reflective blacktop on the outskirts of town.

At this time of night, the streets were empty. He rounded the bend to see the flashing blue lights on the blue, white and neon colored police car.

"What are you doing here, Alistair? I didn't think you received my message" Detective Inspector Rose Campbell stood in front of the house, her strawberry blonde hair whipped around her heart shaped face from the slight breeze. Her lips slightly pursed. To anyone looking on, she might have appeared nonchalant, but he knew the truth. With her shoulders back, and her head tilted to the side, it was as if she was inviting him to come over and catch a whiff of her perfume that had a way of making him forget most things, as well as remember why their relationship didn't work. Thunder boomed, and the storm that was just on his periphery arrived.

"Pretty rough out here, huh?" he answered, and pulled his coat tighter around him. The winter storms had a way of appearing out of nowhere, blowing from the Loch to land. "Thanks for your message and your discretion."

"Well, we haven't had anything like this in couple of generations." Rose, as the Order's supernatural liaison, and the link between the Order and the human world, was a walking lexicon of information. She'd been born to a sup mother and a human father allowing her entrance into both worlds. "Well, don't thank me quite yet. I dare say, something is going on around these parts."

"Something is always happening in this area, as tourists make their way through these historic streets."

"But this is not about tourists."

Their window for him to take a look at the scene would only last so long before the other police officers would show up and begin the human part of investigating.

"Are you going to tell me the details here in the street or take me inside and let me see for myself what's occurred? I am responsible for this area, and any supernatural activity is something that I need to look into."

She nodded her head, "And that is why you are here. With all the caretaking of your latest mewler, I'm surprised you were able to pull yourself away."

Mewler? An interesting term for a new vampire, but he wasn't going to spar with her tonight.

"We all have our talents and uses," he responded.

Alistair wasn't up for her barbed remarks or hurt feelings. There was enough history between them that taking into consideration how she felt and why, were apt to distract him from finding out if a supernatural killed this human, and if so, which one? As this was his territory, he was responsible for keeping it safe, among other things—so is the Order of the Draconian.

"Not a drop of blood found?" he asked.

"No. Looking at her skin, it is practically translucent. And as we know, only mewlers are reckless enough to do something so callous, as they can't control themselves or their appetites. So, how is your recently changed one doing?

"I know you are not suggesting—"

"I'm doing more than suggesting. Evidently, you're harboring a dangerous creature."

Instead of responding, he nodded his head, placed on his shoe covers, and followed Rose into the stone house. The quaint boding had no character inside, but was filled with modern amenities, including a large screen television.

But it was the naked female placed in the center of the sigil that gave him pause. Most would consider the sigil to be reminiscent of witchcraft, but both he and Rose knew it for what it was—the ancient symbol of the Order of Draconian.

"Now I understand why you contacted me"." Alistair sighed. He leaned down next to the woman, and on her neck was indeed the bite mark as that left by a vampire. "That makes no sense, as a mewler would have torn her throat out, and my mewler, who is under my protection, would have ripped it to shreds. This one here was delicately bitten, and every drop lapped up. That speaks of expertise. Additionally, it would not only have been about the blood, but the essence. If you smelled magic here, then this was not the one you are convinced could do this degree of harm."

"Vamps haven't been seen around here in a very long time, Alistair. You know what this could mean?"

Alistair shook his head. "The treaty has not been broken. Those under my protection know that they are not to feed off of humans."

"Knowing and doing are two different things."

"Did you notice any trace of magic when you entered the home? Usually a trace will be left."

Alistair agreed and continued to scrutinize the scene, when he noticed the edge of paper that appeared under the woman's arm.

"Rose," he pointed. "what's that under her arm?"

Rose leaned down and helped to rock the stiff woman's body to the side where they found her laying on a book cover.

"Looks like one of those hot romances," she said, and they stared at the cover.

Alistair didn't worry about the model on the cover, but the female's name: Leslie Love. Can't get any more obvious than that.

"Have you read any of her work?" Rose asked. "I was saddened to hear that she went missing recently. I guess this poor woman felt the same way. Nothing like knowing the author passed away and the series won't continue."

"Series?"

"Yes, she wrote about the Highlands. Romance at its best." Rose must have noticed that her words weren't as contrite and restricted as when she'd started their conversation for she stepped back.

"I've warded this place as long as I can, but soon the other police will be here. Do you know anything about this?"

Alistair wavered. Nothing said a target like having actual evidence with the suspect's name on it at the scene of a crime. Geesh. He glanced around the room and didn't even notice a bookcase with books. He headed from room to room, and with all the shelf space, there weren't any books to be found.

Did the killer bring the book along, or was it a book the victim decided to read?

"You know how it is," Rose continued. "Once bitten by the romance bug, she wasn't going to put that book down even when facing death."

He wasn't sure if Rose spoke from personal experience, or what this one clue meant besides leading to Leslie.

"Have you read this one?"

"Of course." Rose rolled her eyes. She was being honest, almost too honest, as if a spell was working on her forcing her to let down her police officer persona and instead, divulge what he needed to know. For a spell to work on such a powerful hybrid showed that of sustained and powerful magic.

"If I'm right, that's the one about the *völva*, women versed well in our ancient magic and ways." As she spoke she slowed down. "You don't think this is a clue do you? That this Leslie Love knew or is a part of this world, our world?"

The humans will do a toxicology report. They'd discover if something else was at work, but völva knew how to heal and kill, which meant that Leslie, back at the castle, knew those things too.

Could she be the one responsible for this murder, and maybe not even know it?

# Chapter 19

**LESLIE**

I lost track of time. Days and nights mixed in my room where I chose to stay. Hidden behind thick curtains, many might have enjoyed this new world, but not me. Hate might have been a strong word, but it wasn't strong enough for me.

"If you can put this on, his Lordship will be happy to see you up and at it."

The dress reminded me of what it must have been like to have new money—clothes that felt expensive, which fit perfectly. Rich material in a pale periwinkle on a plush hanger was thrust my way.

She kept her distance, and I was to accept that I couldn't kill her. Unfortunately, that was the thought throughout the day. How to kill and drain her dry. This thirst fought against the rising hate of the situation too. I didn't care that I was now in what must have been a Scottish castle based on the decor.

"Uh, I usually don't find clothes that fit so easily," I muttered, hiding my thoughts.

"No worries, these are just for you."

She then handed me a pair of black high heels that fit as if made just for me.

I painted on a smile and waited for the door to click closed.

"Gran," I loudly whispered. "Gran."

"No need to shout, dear. Aren't you happy I was able to find this great man, a lord, to help out?"

"How is it that you can appear and disappear?"

"I don't know. Haven't really figured that out, but this place is just perfect for your next Macleod book. The ceiling height, the grounds; I've seen it all."

"And the strange vibe I'm getting here?"

"Well, you don't have the best instinct. This place is incredible. Better than being on that ship, I tell you. You wanted to get out of there anyway. This is definitely an improvement."

I slowly put the outfit on. "Have you seen anyone else here?"

"Anyone else?" Gran stopped to think. "This place is filled with people. A complete unique society."

"Whew," I sighed. "I was starting to get worried." I was sure she heard the annoyance in my voice.

"They are all just supernatural, some even dead, but you don't have a thing to concern yourself with."

"What!" My hands stopped trying to button up the pearl-button sleeves. "I'm surrounded by things I don't understand. This doesn't make sense. The supernatural world doesn't really exist. It can't." I shook my head in disbelief, knowing full well what she said was true, but it was easier for me to live in denial.

"You know, you get this way when you are upset—all scientific. And there are tons of reasons to consider your current situation as not being optimal, but just because you can't see it or didn't know it existed, doesn't mean that it can't be true."

"This is not just believing in Santa Claus, this is a dragon!"

"It's not the first time. This place is perfect for us. Come, you don't want to leave his Lordship waiting." She paused. "You know, I could use a word of thanks from you too. This is the perfect spot for you to make your return to publishing, immersed in your story; you're meeting a handsome man."

"A mistake." I seethed. "I didn't need a man, or a happy ever after."

"You close yourself off so much from love. He will not be your next mistake. He's too handsome for that."

"You don't get it." I began to shake with anger. "This existence for me is sheer terror. I am a stranger in my own body." The angrier I became, I felt my canines descend. "Plus, I'll take your word on that. I have a way of making good men turn bad."

"No, more like bad men turn worse."

I guess I should have taken that as a positive. At least she didn't say that I made them into *the* worst.

"This one here, he is different and in such a good way. Just you wait and see. He is going to sweep you off your feet and then I can finally see those grandbabies I've been waiting for."

"Oh my god, I barley know the man, and you're trying to plan a wedding."

"No dear, I didn't say wedding. I said grandchildren. You can't live in a cave forever, and this man is like a male Aphrodite. I might be dead, but if I had ovaries, they would quiver."

"Ew, Gran."

A fresh wave of rage punched me. I could feel the invisible chains that held me in place. My body refused to listen to my commands of rise and run away from this place.

I didn't ask to be turned into this monster, tied to this new life that I knew nothing about. When I left for vacation, the highest chance of something going wrong was that I could walk away with a yeast infection from the freaking pool chlorine, but to not be able to return to my life? Everything I'd built, taken from me in an instant. Every accolade voided, friendship erased, and dreams now crushed.

I clenched and unclenched my fists.

Gran stared at me.

"The rage is normal, I hear," Gran said, but I ignored her. She'd allowed this to be done to me. Of course, she wouldn't have wanted to be tied to a dead body floating up and down the coast, since her ring of light was situated on my hand, but that didn't mean that I could ever forgive her for this.

"I did what I thought was best. I've watched so many of my loved ones' pass, but you are different. We actually have a relationship. You can hear the inflection of my voice and not wait for me to communicate with flickering lights, books that might move on their own, or boo sounds. You see me."

I whipped my head around. "But you stole everything from me due to your selfishness."

"You love the Highlands, dear."

"No, I loved the apartment in New York. I loved the city. What am I supposed to do out here? Milk cows, sheer sheep? Hell, no one thought about me while making their decisions, just what they could get from me."

"Why don't you put all of that frustration to good use. Now that you're immortal, your body can move like a machine."

"I don't want to move like a machine, wear incredibly tight leather and rock a katana. I'm not a character in some freaking urban fantasy tale. This is my life."

Gran folded her hands in her lap, and stopped floating to take a seat. "What would you have me do?"

"Help me find my way. I can't go this alone, but I also don't know anything about what it means to be... this... this thing. If you were truly alive, I would have killed you by now."

"That is the thing, Leslie. I think you need to find a way, an outlet to let go of all that rage."

"How?"

"What did you want to do when you were a child?"

"Play football?"

"No, not that."

"I wanted to be Wonder Woman."

Gran frowned. "That is a start, but you also wanted to be a wrestler, remember? You could surely do something with that."

"I was eight, and it was the eighties."

"Well, you did something then, and I expect you to do it now. What were we supposed to do? Let you die? If you are dead set on having a pity party about it—go walk into the sunlight and get it over with, but I will not take you pouting around like a little brat when someone does something good for you. So, put on the damn dress, get downstairs and thank your host. Tonight, let him wine and dine you, and maybe you can let your hair down, for once."

"I'm not having sex with him."

"Pfft. I'm not asking about that, but I promise not to think less of you if you do. You will have to see his wonderful face, and a body that will encourage you to do bad things with him.

You remember the time I sent you to that bondage workshop for the third Macleod book?"

"Gran"."

"Well, just imagine all of those kinky things you could do." She began to hum.

"I told you about it, but not because I wanted your expertise in case I met someone."

"Just promise me, you won't give him the cold shoulder. He is too fine to be given the cold shoulder to."

"If you say that one more time, I'm going to take the ring off and put it in my pocket," I said and raised my hand. There were times when she enjoyed the game of romance way too much, and I wasn't sure if I was up to playing with her whispering in my ear.

"You don't have to worry about that. I don't think I'd be able to sneak in on him anyway. He seems to have a knack for seeing the undead."

I collapsed back on the chaise. "This is all insane. First freezing in the sea, and now playing dress up to meet a lord who can see the dead—and he's a dragon.

"Well, there are worse things, dear," Gran said.

"What's that?"

"You could be dead too, and I sort of promised you to him. So you might as well have at him."

"You did what?" I screamed.

"I needed him to save you. And he seemed lonely enough. I guess something about a desperate woman dying called to him." She shrugged her shoulders.

I pushed up from the chaise and headed toward the door, sucked my teeth and clenched my jaw. Unsteady on my feet, I wobbled on the high heels down the long hallway. Large painted portraits hung on the wall that I hadn't noticed previously. At my speed, they were a simple blur.

"Welcome to his lordship's home," Gran said. "Do you think all of these women are his ex-lovers? If so, boy does he have a type. Look, if we stay long enough, he might be able to paint one of you too. Wouldn't that be romantic?"

"I just want to make it through this meet and greet, climb back up to a bed, and pull the covers over my head. If I'm lucky, he'll have a stake. Whatever shenanigans you have planned will have to wait for another day."

Long shadows covered up what I assumed to be perfectly painted and beautiful women on the walls, and as my gaze drifted, I didn't expect them to land on the man waiting in the hallway with his arms crossed. He was dressed in a tailored black suit, with the collar of his black shirt slightly undone. I took a gulp.

Freaking hormones.

"Did you hear a lot of that?" I asked him.

"No worries. I've been accused of more than just collecting paintings." He turned away and assumed I should follow. "Come, Leslie."

I took a step. Not like I had a lot of choice.

Damn him for taking that away from me.

# Chapter 20

**ALISTAIR**

"Are the runes in place?" Alistair asked Rose, who stood to his right.

Seated on his throne in the great hall on a dais, with Gillianbusti loudly snorting beside him, Alistair considered his options.

With the woman's death, he must now speak to the community and advise them of what this could mean.

Within the estate, Rose still gave him due deference as the Lord of the Order, the ruler and that which kept their worlds safe.

"Yes, my Lord. Today we must make sure that everything is taken care of. This place likes to devour the ladies who arrive here, but even more, they will make it that no one can enter." Alistair wiped his brow. The last thing he wanted to be reminded of was that if Leslie stayed she'd be put in danger, and if she left, he'd be forever stuck to enjoy the night, but never the daylight, as his bite had connected their souls.

And it also didn't help that her hostility was growing more and more each day. She'd need to work out, but also be introduced to this new world where she would be under his protection.

He scanned the crowd and wondered. Who could have killed the girl in the village? He couldn't get rid of the image of the deceased girl out of his head.

"Make sure that everyone is visible, dear Rose. We don't want to scare our guests. We need them."

He watched Killian make his way through the throng of people to stand at this right.

Alistair picked up his staff and banged it against the floor, silencing the room.

The growing ruckus in the grand room wasn't what he'd expected to encounter when he'd called the meeting. On most days, everyone got along swell, but this was not most days.

"Should we not be concerned about this human you've brought here?" asked one gentleman, but it wasn't just that one question, but the question of many for several nodded their heads.

Alistair tried not to frown. Even he had his trepidation, but there was no reason to let that woman die.

"In this Order, as created by the gods, our mission is to be a place for those like us, and we have accepted the two women, Myrtle, and her granddaughter, Leslie, into our abode. Both have not been properly introduced. You will meet them today and welcome them as I have welcomed each of you.

"The change is not always one of birth. Some of us here have been different since we took our first breath, while others have transitioned and in death, found this place to be their beacon; and yet others—"

"But this one is different. She's a vampire. They haven't been in these parts in centuries."

"Calm down. Now," Alistair said. "This woman is a vampire, but also my mate."

He heard Rose's sharp inhale. "As I am her sire. What you do to her, you do to me. She is not to be harmed—not a hair on her head or hide."

"But I thought he was only to marry the seer," Rose whispered.

"Interesting games the gods play," Killian responded.

"You created a vampire, but did not tell me of this at the scene, Alistair," Rose bristled. "It is possible that this abomination has killed."

Alistair shook his head, but he watched the idea grow steam as those in the crowd began to nod in agreement. "By creating her, you have created a quagmire for vampires that are outlawed. They almost decimated the area, feeding on supes and humans alike."

"Do you dare question my authority, Rose?"

"I am a wielder, and the magic required to keep this place safe, I can also wield. You have brought forth a blight, and in doing so, you will bring attention to us, and cause us all harm. That is not thinking in the best interest of our kind."

Peter, the herbalist and mage, moved forward to stand in front of Alistair. "You are all quite wrong about this Leslie. She has a strong fortitude like I've never seen. Even more, his Lordship was only gifted his ability once. If she is forced to die, then you will also kill him, as their souls are tethered together. And surely, you do not wish death on the one who has harbored you and granted you a place of peace."

Killian slapped down his hand on Alistair's shoulder, and stepped forward too.

"There is more that you don't know. The seer is not just a prophecy, but for the great battle, she will be needed so that we may win, and stand with the gods at Ragnarok. I have spoken to the other orders, and each of their seers have spoken of her. She is blessed by the gods, chosen by them for him, and for us. We do them and her a disservice to not allow the lass a chance to prove herself."

"What can you tell us about the murder in town"?" Peter asked.

Rose then stepped forward. "The body was drained of blood, and after initial testing, I located traces of henbane at the scene. Henbane is used by the seers to kill."

"It sounds as if you are ready to bring her before the magistrate for this?" Killian asked.

Alistair rose. "Here I am just that." He banged his staff again against the floor. "Grace, I pronounce, she is under the protection of the Order."

Rose sucked in her cheeks, bowed and stepped back. "As you say, my Lord."

It wasn't every day that he allowed recently turned, and unvetted, to pass over the threshold into their inner sanctum. Consequences could be dire. Although last night, he'd allowed the dragon to come out, the beast still barely rested under the surface. God or not, being one with the dragon, as decided by Freyja was not what he'd wanted for his future. How did his dragon skillset help Asgard? He didn't know. All that he understood was that a beast came forward once every full moon, and in that time, bad things happened.

Things he couldn't quite remember.

"Bring the women forth," Alistair declared.

# Chapter 21

**LESLIE**

From the back of the room we listened and watched it all. Talk about being disliked. Seemed like vampires were as badly hated as carpal tunnel, brussel sprouts, and assholes.

The place was strange. Not only did it have the magnificent aroma of fresh cloves everywhere, but the air felt like that NASA grade oxygen, at least from what I could remember from space camp eons ago. It was cool and refreshing. My lungs breathed it in, and did a little happy dance recognizing it for what it was—pure, delightful air.

In a crowd of humanoid, dragon-like creatures, the colors of forest green illuminated around the shoulders of the one who Alistair identified as Rose. Her ears were pointy, and she stood tall and lean. I knew right away that she was not an ordinary person. She was more beautiful than almost any woman I'd ever seen.

"What is this place?" I wondered aloud and all turned to look at me.

"Psst, Gran," I whispered, "Do you see all of this too"?"

Gran, of course, saw everything—that was the great thing about being a ghost. "Oh, child," Gran responded. "I think you are going to have to be careful about which rooms you enter. What if each of these rooms takes you to one of the different realms, the nine worlds"?"

"That is outrageous."

"Look around you. We're surrounded by supernaturals," she whispered.

I felt Alistair's stare heavy on me, as he watched my every movement. He brazenly cleared his throat. "Dearly beloved, please welcome your new kin, Myrtle and Leslie"."

Huddled together, Gran took my hand and we walked up front to wear Alistair stood. Just as his gaze was heavy, so was the disapproval of all of those around us. They shot bullets with their stern stares.

"It's great to be here," I said with a broad smile. I wasn't sure if he could tell that I was lying, but it seemed plausible enough to me that something like that could happen.

He crossed his arms.

I don't have Daddy issues. Those days disappeared a long time ago, somewhere between age twenty-five, and me finding out that I didn't need an agent to publish my first book. Imagine my surprise on knowing that there were tons of men interested in offering me a free ride. They didn't care what my hopes and dreams were, only if I was willing to bed them. They didn't love me, and I refused to love them.

*This is a mistake. I don't belong here, and although I am very thankful for your saving me from the depths of death, I'm confused.* Words I should have said, but instead, I began to ramble about the interior design. How it felt like a college dorm or old age community, and how I couldn't wait to meet everyone individually.

Maybe I shouldn't have expected a warm reception, but I still expected something, and something is exactly what I got. Up until now, Gran might have said that things which were too good to be true, usually were. And Although Alistair was attempting to make my transition to this side as painless as possible, this was like getting my wisdom teeth removed. For the first thirty seconds, you could a pin drop, all the while the pet boar snorted and snotted.

"Is it me, or is something off kilter?" Gran asked.

The crowd turned their backs on us, and dispersed without a word.

I didn't think that was the normal way for a meeting to be dismissed, in fact, I found it profoundly rude.

"Excuse them," said the man to Alistair's left. He stretched out his hand. "It's going to take time for everyone to adjust to your being here. I'm Killian." He was a handsome man in that wilderness sort of way—like he'd just had a dashing run in the mountains, running with wolves.

"It's an adjustment for all." I took his hand, and gasped, then morphed into a wolf.

# Chapter 22

**ALISTAIR**

With the meeting ended, Alistair returned to his chambers to think.

Responsibility weighed heavily on his shoulders. He paced. Just as the prophecy declared, as the seer, she operated almost like a sponge, able to mimic the talents of anyone she touches.

He picked up the dog-eared novel and began again to read the tale of Ivan, the Viking. It wasn't enough that Ivan couldn't be with his people in Norway, but now had to set up a homestead in the hostile territory of the Highlands. He flipped through the pages, choosing the romance novel over that of his current situation.

Ivan reminded him of who he used to be, before he'd taken the call. How he'd slaughtered in the name of the gods; the million reasons he'd embraced becoming the dragon he'd always been.

His chamber door flew open, and Rose stomped in. "You didn't listen to anything I said, Alistair," Rose said. "What you witnessed here tonight is an anomaly. Dangerous. You know what a seer of such powers will do."

Alistair cleared his throat, put the book to the side, and shook his head. "Rose, I expect your next report forthwith as to any news regarding this crime. You're dismissed."

He ignored her accusations. There was too much riding on this for him not to act.

"You know you could always send her away? Or to another Order, but if she is indeed slaughtering humans, there will be nowhere that you can send her. In effect, you might have just signed your own death sentence." Rose curtsied and left him to consider the options as to what could be transpiring.

Alistair essentially assumed the same. But was the risk of being stuck here worth it? What Freyja wanted she usually got, and although he couldn't see the other side of the equation, he knew she must be up to something.

A knock on his door distracted him, for there Leslie stood, bundled up from head to toe.

"I thought you were heading to bed, Ms. Love?"

She smiled. "I would have done the same, but I had one question before I could sleep."

"Yes?" He didn't want to answer any questions. He'd saved her from drowning and certain death shouldn't that have been enough? "But I cannot guarantee that I will answer."

She nodded. "That is fair enough." She cleared her throat, pulled back her shoulders, took a deep breath and then paused." "I don't know how to begin this."

He moved his energy outward and prodded until her body began to relax, watching as her muscles eased, and her jaw unclenched.

"Is that better?"

"No," she said and shook her head. "I have a request. Please, stay out of my mind. I do not wish for you to read my thoughts."

"Are you sure?" In all of his years, he'd never had a woman complain. Most wanted him to know what they desired before they could utter a word, as if he were a magical genie, and they were to be rewarded for thinking it.

He smiled in return. "I will respect your wishes. But I must also make a request, since I know that you are Ms. Love, I have a proposition for you."

"Uh-oh," she said, catching herself, he watched her cover her mouth with her hands.

"Not one of those, but my dear servant girl, Rose, is a great fan of your work, and since you write stories of the Highlands, I insist that you make use of your time here and do the research you need to create your next tale."

"Wait. What? You want me to write a book while staying here. A book takes more than a couple of days."

"Yes, I'm sure it does. But here, you can soak in all of that Highland magic and it can spark your next tale. You wouldn't want to disappoint your fans by not having that next book finished, right?"

He watched her emotions play across her face—she seemed to war against herself, but he refused to look closer. Whatever she had to say, from now on, she must say it to him and not simply think it.

"How long can I stay?"

"You are an American and have ninety days. No problem without a visa. What could be better?"

"Are you serious?"

"Yes. My estate, my home, staff and I are at your service to help you in any way possible, to maybe even inspire your muse." He took a step forward to close the space between them.

He didn't know why—why she beckoned him—called to him, but right now, he had no desire to see her walk away. Although he wanted to be alone, and feared that something might transpire, he was a god and would protect her as only a man could.

He leaned in closer, and she walked backwards until the wall was at her back. He stood toe-to-toe with her. "So, what is your answer, dear lass?"

# Chapter 23

**LESLIE**

He'd asked for a private audience. I'd thought it might an introductory lesson: How to be a supernatural? Nope. He might as well have been sitting in his overly stuffed office chair, brooding, while swinging a pair of handcuffs. He gave me every impression that a supernatural jail awaited.

I shook my hands, hoping that such a simple motion might cause them to stop tingling. I paced.

"If you keep pacing like that, you are going to wear a hole in my carpet"," Alistair finally said.

"This is why I left college behind years ago. This "oh, look what she said, did, didn't do, but we have to blame someone" crapola."

"Calm down. You're walking so fast that you're beginning to blur," he said.

"I guess it must be that super speed," I guffawed.

I wanted him to enclose me in his arms, but instead it was like he was shoving thorns under my fingernails.

"If you want to accuse me of something, then I want you to take me there."

He shook his head before I could even get my question out. He slumped back in his chair. "Your blood lust is too great. I can't let you outside these warded walls, for if you leave, I can't guarantee what you might do, or attack."

He couldn't know that I had the inner strength and perseverance of a river, and right now, he was my rock. One way or another, I was going to find out the truth, and neither he nor his cronies were going to make it otherwise.

"And who is this person that I was supposed to have killed? I might not be able to leave, but I can do a google search"," I asked Alistair.

"Google?"

"Oh my gosh, how are you living without Wi-Fi? I need to bring you up to date, just like you need to make sure that I can acclimate to this new world."

He must have been holding on to the past with an iron fist, but he didn't know that satellites were taking pictures from above, that everything was only a mouse click away, and especially that life was more than just this archaic Order.

"You might find my life here different, but it is this way for a reason. Those things are purposely outside of these walls, and I hope you will respect that."

It certainly explained why I'd yet to find a phone in the castle to make a call. Note to self: get a cell phone.

"I don't even know anyone here, and now I'm supposed to have tracked someone down, followed them home, and drained them dry? And of course, I carry my books with me wherever I go. I'm sure if you give me a moment I can make a paperback appear from thin air."

I couldn't help the sarcasm in my voice. This felt like high school. Let's get the new girl ousted before she's able to snag the cool football player. Okay, the only analogy is that he wasn't cool, and this wasn't high school, but even worse than that, this was supposed to be a sanctuary. It seemed somewhat spoiled now.

"Her name was Bridget McCullough, age twenty-two. She lived in the village, and was preparing to enter the local university in the coming semester. She'd come here from Edinburgh."

"That's a good beginning. Now, take my hand and lead me to the scene."

He shook his head. "Your anger does not negate what you could have done. I must investigate all angles, even the most unlikely ones. Just because you show no signs of recognition, doesn't mean that you didn't indeed do something quite horrible."

I sighed. My hands were shaking, my canines began to descend. My vision began to cloud. "I have to get out of here."

"I don't think that is a good idea. Your life has changed, and there is a high likelihood that should you leave and walk in the daylight that you will burn. Vampires are creatures of the night after all.

For one, I didn't care what he thought. His words were not going to hold me back from learning truth. The only thing I had to do was keep the blood lust in check, and find out where this Bridget lived.

"Well, it seems that no one really likes to think around here, just assume." I rushed past him, through the door to find Gran waiting.

"It took you long enough. I thought I was going to have to start to prepare your funeral," she said.

"Me too. What did you find out from talking to the others?" I didn't want to worry her about what Alistair had said. He'd do anything to keep me here, even if it is not where I wanted to be.

"No one really wanted to talk to me, but I do have a way of making people respond. So, I swiped a phone. I see you using this all the time, and the groundskeeper had his just lying around. Maybe you can find what you need through a simple punching of keys."

I shrugged. "I wished it would be that easy, but ..."

"If not, I might have another way." She then pulled out a raven's feather.

"What's that?"

"I overheard Kenneth who was talking to Sam and Della about someone they are calling the seer. Well, the seer is different than a normal supernatural and able to do different things. So, since we are new here, and I can't do anything, I thought it must be you. I need you to do the ritual with the henbane. Utter your prayer chant while holding this and let's see if you can shift into your spirit animal."

I knew in Norse mythology, there was a possibility that people had a totem animal or what others called a fylgja.

"I guess I need to get to the garden downstairs and see what they might have."

"No need, I was hoping you'd say yes." Then she produced a pouch of henbane."

Clutching the feather, and lighting the henbane, I waited.

"You need to focus on that raven," Gran said.

I didn't feel like I could connect with this ceremony—I was different. Everything felt wrong, as if I tried to free myself from invisible tangles, and webs.

"If you don't find out the truth, Leslie, they are going to try to pin this murder on you. You know what they say, the dead can't speak."

A thought formed. "But what if they could? Come, concentrate your energy with my own, and let's see what we can make happen together. Maybe we can find Bridget."

I closed my eyes, concentrated on my breathing, and the feel of the black feather in my hand. I'd been searching for Bridget, but I never expected that when I opened my mouth only a caw would come out.

"You did it," Gran said. "You found your spirit animal."

I bowed my head and saw spinney black feet and black feathers. My feathers puffed out in fear.

"There is no need to be afraid"," she said. I chirped as she yanked a feather from my wing.

She walked to the window and pulled back the drawn curtains. Luckily it was still night, but dawn would be here soon. I hopped on the ledge, then Gran lifted me up and tossed me out the opened window as if I were a part of a dove release at wedding. "Now, go find out the truth."

FLYING WASN'T AS EASY as I thought it would be. After a pair of false starts and after hitting a tree, I learned how to use my wings, it was like soaring with helium.

After what felt like hours, I finally located the address provided from the internet. From the outside, the house seemed normal, but once inside, I felt the evil that lurked there. Although I wasn't sure if it were possible, I concentrated on my shape and again, transformed in a cloud of henbane back to my human form.

I'd read enough police procedurals to be dangerous. But I had a talent the police didn't.

"Bridget," I called out. I don't know what I expected to happen. Maybe a chair sliding across the room, or maybe the air would shimmer, and she'd appear.

Yeah, that would have been too simple.

Instead, the sigil appeared, and began to glow with bright purple light shooting up from the middle. My eyes rolled into the back of my head, my body began to seize and quake midair. This was magic, a strong magic that had entered this room.

Colors began to splash all around me, and out walked Bridget.

"You've come to speak with me," she asked.

I couldn't move, stuck in the light.

"You shouldn't have. You've placed yourself in great danger."

"I already am," I said through clenched teeth.

"Then the truth I shall show you. Every ghost has a piece of what happened, but can only see from their perspective." She reached out and touched me, and the scene in my mind went from technicolor to black and white. The scenes bled into each other, from her simply preparing a cup of tea, to a figure she couldn't see grabbing her from behind. The smell of wheat wafted from his skin, mixed with a musty or earthy smell.

"Bridget, did you know him?"

"No, I'd only lived here for a couple of weeks." Her face dropped its ethereal glow and was replaced with extreme sadness. It wrapped around me like a blanket, and held me down despite my struggle. Her emotions caused my own eyes to well.

"Where did you live before?" I struggled to ask.

"On the property adjacent to the castle."

"That castle"?" Scotland had tons of castles. What was the likelihood that she was a tenet of Alistair's lands?

"Yes. I'd wanted to stay, but strange things began to happen and I knew that it was better for me to leave than to waste my time there. I guess I was wrong."

Her final words faded, and I dropped to the ground with a heavy thud. She wasn't a stranger to the castle, but had connections to it. Connections that existed way before me. Although my book might be the calling card, this wasn't about me, but about someone else at the castle for sure.

# Chapter 24

**LESLIE**

I couldn't quite get the bird transformation thing to work in order to get back to the castle.

The village wasn't that far away from it, though, but wow, talk about the heebee jeebies. I could feel someone watching me,. Goosebumps. Maybe it was because I was a stranger here, but, although the roads were mostly empty, besides an occasional car, and no one meandered around, it seemed that the town was indeed deserted.

The sun was rising, and the higher it got, the more tired I became. Where it landed, it then began to burn.

Crapola, I'd forgotten sunblock. I pulled my collar up to protect my neck, and walked looking downward, peering through the spaces in-between my curls.

"Don't burst out in flames. Don't burst out in flames."

Over the years I'd watched many vampire movies, and that is what I knew to be true. They were creatures of the night. What in the name of the gods gave me the idea to go out in and stay out while the sun was shining?

Needing a reprieve, I ducked into the telephone booth – I'd never been so happy to see a big red box.

There was only one number I knew: Claudine's. She'd know who to inform.

The phone rang three times before she picked up with her thick morning voice.

"Hello?" she answered.

"Claudine, it's me, Leslie."

"Why are you calling me? Better yet, where are you? Your schedule must have you super busy. I haven't seen you in a few days... You were supposed to have that breakfast this morning. You know, Maurice is never going to take you back with you ditching paying customers."

"Well, Maurice can shove it since someone threw me over the rail last night."

"Very funny."

"But I'm telling you the truth. I could swear Donovan did this. He didn't like that I wasn't into him."

"Shh, don't say that too loudly. He's right here snoring away."

"Aagh, you slept with him."

"Well, I didn't get much sleep," she giggled.

"You're going to giggle when he tried to kill me"?"

"I tried to kill him too, hay."

"You are a fool"."

"I was doing ready for the world on him, backwards cow girl, getting my model fill. Girl, you just don't know."

I could only laugh at her reaction. That was Claudine, not a serious bone in her body. Of course, I wouldn't want it any other way.

"You don't sound too concerned. I'm being serious."

"You're alive, and okay?" I could hear the laughter leaving her voice as my words settled.

Claudine was a good older sister. She could pick and tease, knew how to have a good time too. But there are two things you don't tell an arias: that you ate all of their favorite foods, and of course, that you hurt their kin. Now, it's not about them not being able to hurt kinfolks. That pleasure was for family members only. She could be a real meanie to me, for sure, but she didn't like it when someone else did that.

"Can you hold on for a minute?" she asked.

I held the phone to my ear, and just heard a sharp cry, and thump. "Now get your crusty ass out of my bed, and stay there until I call ship security on you. No one hurts my sister you fucking moron."

"Please!" I heard him plea.

In my mind, Claudine had kicked him out of her bed, and probably poked him with something to wake him up – something sharp and pointy.

"What are you doing to him?" I asked.

"Make sure he doesn't slither away. Snake. I'm going to turn you in to security and maybe they can then throw you over board.

"Hold on."

I heard an alarm blaring, as she must have pressed the emergency call button.

"I mean, don't get me wrong, he was cute and all, but no, that is just nasty, and stupid. He's like moronic without reason." Her voice lowered for a moment, and she leaned away from the phone. "And your sex was not that good. Your body is a hot advertisement but your moves are lacking. If I wanted something that could just lay there, well, there are toys for that. Damn. Attempted murdering psycho."

"Are we really talking about this?"

"You go after men in suits instead of men who work those fast food jobs. They know how to make me meow."

"You just like free fries."

"I like free anything, and right now, I like free D—"

"Don't even. I didn't call to find out if your fantasy came true last night. I hope you get tested when you get back to shore. Don't know what that bag of fleas has."

"One thing I can say is that he was packing a potato or maybe a sock. Whatever it was, it thudded out, like a wham! He is a lot sexier on those covers. Do you think they do Photoshop?"

"Thanks for asking, Claudine. I am quite okay. Found a haunted billionaire to watch over me until I can figure out what I'm supposed to do."

"Just sit on his face and your problems will be gone."

"Bye, Claudine."

I could only take so much of her shenanigans.

"Woah, but how am I going to reach you? Serious though, are you okay? I got this piece of shit here, and I might just poke out his eye with this fish fork. I am so mad right now, and I don't like being mad, Leslie. That is what this cruise was supposed to be about – relaxation, no strings, and instead I have to deal with this."

Only my sister could make my being pushed overboard about her.

"I'll call you back once I figure it all out,"

"But where did you wash up at?"

"A town not far from Inbhir." Since I didn't speak Gaelic, my pronunciation didn't actually sound like it should have, for sure.

"Sounds like paradise." I heard her yawn, followed by a knock on the door

"I'll let you know once I figure that part out, too."

"They're here. I'm going to make sure they lock him up."

Placing the receiver back in the cradle, I knew Claudine was a true fool and probably had stabbed Donovan with a fish fork. He should be happy she didn't grab the lobster cracker.

I turned and stepped back out into the street. The air around me twinkled and the cobblestone street, once empty, quickly filled with men and women carrying baskets with parcels. Some wore modern day clothes, while others were dressed in women's plaid, belted.

"Are you the latest woman from the castle"?" she asked, pointing to where I'd just been. "I'll never understand why he doesn't have a telephone after all of this time."

"You sound like you know him."

"I know him and I also know women like you. But you will just be like all of the others. I barely escaped from his grasp. He would have killed me."

I called bullshit on that one. She might have been his type. She might even have visited the castle, but he wasn't a killer. I'd visited enough jails and prisons to know the truth of it all.

"Does this warning work with all of the other girls?"

"Some heed my warning, but you are not going to be one of them, I take it."

I could feel the jealousy. "You have history with him? Or is it that you want to have history with him?"

"You don't understand what you're doing. He will never give you what you need because you are not his ex-wife. She's marked him as her territory."

"I don't need to listen to this."

"Watch. He'll try to make you into her—the clothes, the hair, the perfume. You'll smell like expensive lavender on a summer day. It will be her scent, because unlike you, he can't have her."

I yanked my arm out of her grasp, yet she continued. "Don't you want to hear about the bodies that he's buried due to his delicacies? All of the ex-girlfriends, those who couldn't get away? That place is haunted and there are numerous dead bodies piling up around him."

I raced away as fast as my feet could carry me. I didn't know anything about him. Maybe I should have just been relieved that I was able to leave the castle's grounds without him being aware. I'd been sent there to find out the truth. Was the truth that women who got involved with him died? Or worse, were murdered?

Paranoia scratched until it clawed me.

He had been too perfect.

And perfection could be deadly.

"A serial killer is loose, I tell you, and he is connected to that abominable castle."

# Chapter 25

**LESLIE**

"You did what?" Alistair yelled.

I'd returned to find him in a less content mood than before, but I did disobey his orders. Seemed like I had an issue with assholes being in positions of authority.

Sure, I didn't expect for him to be happy that I left, but when I'd arrived back at the castle, the guards had escorted me straight to his office. I couldn't expect him to figure out this mess for me, but I could provide him with the answers that he didn't have.

"I will not be blamed for something that I didn't do. With the gods as my witness, if I am going to go down, I will set this entire Order on fire and make it crumble along with me."

"You are threatening this Order?"

I didn't know what I wanted from him, from them, but I knew that I wasn't going to allow myself to be framed.

My thoughts were a muddled mess. A toss of the coin could mean hate or love; pleasure or undeniable pain. My teeth descended. I felt that magnetic pull between us, and I pulled back against it. I stopped myself from pulling on his shirt, but just barely.

"This has nothing to do with me, but with you. Being here will put me in more danger than I was when you rescued me."

"Leave us," he ordered the guards.

"What do you mean?"

"Bridget used to live on your lands. She used to interact with the castle and its tenants. If you expect me to choose you over me, it will not happen. You are my sire, but I am still me. No matter how magnetic you may be, I will not be silenced by your brooding."

"I am the master of this Order, and you are my subject to do as I compel you to," he practically growled.

He was so focused on ruling that he didn't see what was standing before him. I'd just told him that someone killed one of his prior tenants, but instead of asking questions, he was butt hurt about my disobeying him, as if it was okay to kill people, drain them, and then have tons of evidence of foul play stacked up against him.

Men could be such idiots sometimes.

"Shush, we shall discuss this later, as now I must try to clean up what you've done," he said. "What you did was against the rules, and this treaty. You left without knowing them, but still, you left."

"What do you mean?" I caught my rage before it could snowball into something that could annihilate the entire room.

"Simply put, you have given them an in to have me ousted by proving that I have no control over you. A loud tap on the door, and in walked Rose, as if on cue. She didn't even throw me a glance.

"If you wish to rule," she began, "then you need to learn how. It is more than just your being the largest beast."

“Taking sides”?” Alistair countered.

“No, not this time. Maybe I should take over since evidently, I have a better understanding of the threat against us. You are too busy worrying about your reputation, and sniffing your latest recruit, than the actual murder of innocents.”

“I have been appointed by the gods, and there is nothing that you can do about it.”

“And I can take it all away, Alistair. I could make you bend and bow.” She produced a magical orb and in that orb, it showed me walking around Bridget’s house from room to room.

“She was there.”

“Yes, but only today,” I began. Alistair’s scathing glance shut me up.

“Impossible. Our wards are too strong for a mewler to overcome. Only the true killer could have returned, and I think I know the truth even better than you do, Alistair. The question is: What will it cost you for me to remain mum about it”?”

Blackmailed, that’s what it meant for Alistair now, and I watched it play out.

*You are not to say a word, as she is power hungry, you will only make things worse.*

I nodded my head.

“You never should have brought her here and now she will pay the price for breaking the rules.”

“I don’t have to say anything,” I said, as if prompted from the beyond. “I’ll show you.” Tossing down the henbane, the incorporeal figure of Bridget appeared.

“You again?“ she asked. “Are you not going to let me rest?”

“First, you just need to let us know something.”

"You are all quite foolish. He is currently doing to someone else, what he did to me, and you argue about rules, treaties, and politics. Instead, why not use all of that energy to potentially save another from my same fate."

"What heresy is this? I'm going to call the guards back in and then this will all be over, Alistair. Do the right thing, and turn her over."

Alistair nodded his head. "Guards, take Leslie away."

# Chapter 26

**LESLIE**

I hadn't felt this awful since I'd had the flu, complicated by pneumonia. I'd been put into the adult version of time out—locked in my room and unable to leave.

*Come to me.* The voice I didn't want to hear seemed to awaken me. But it wasn't clearly Alistair.

Why should I be expected to carry this burden? My body warred with me. Death might have been better. It wasn't that I had so much to do here that my life couldn't have just ended. Dreams destroyed, loneliness, what did I have to live for besides my Gran? I guess she might have felt the same way. She reached out to me, and touched my hand.

She squeezed it tightly. "Baby girl, I'd do anything to make it so that you didn't have to walk away, walk into the light. I needed you to stay. To imagine being here with you, well, I just couldn't. You can call me selfish—hell, I can't imagine what this is going to cause. But I'll be there with you every step of the way.

"The idea of feeding on someone repulses me," I sobbed. "I've watched enough vampire movies to know how this ends—no more sunlight, or true love. What sort of existence will this be?"

"That is what we shall find out. You're not in this alone. Just a baby, a mewler."

I nodded my head as if understanding, but I couldn't grasp this change so easily. There wasn't just heaven and hell after that final heartbeat, but a space in-between, and this seemed to be it.

"I think I just need to rest some, Gran. This is taking a lot out of me." I shimmied down back under the covers. Alone, I needed to be alone.

Gran had never left me, and I wasn't sure if she knew how to just walk away now that her body had substance again.

She patted me on the head, and I heard the door close.

With my eyes closed, a scene formed in my mind that made little to no sense to me.

I walked on dirt floors in a long narrow building. Exposed timbers, and walls that appeared to be made of sod. Looking up, I stared at the thatched roof. Minimum light shone through, but there was a fire which burnt in the stone hearth. Built-in benches rested along the walls, and around the fire; those I recognized as family, stood. I moved through the scene following that of the young man before me.

His mother tended to her cooking, a smile on her face, while his father, a burly man built like a boulder, bounced a young baby on his knee.

"Alistair," his father raised his hand and waved him over.

"Yes father," he said and took a seat. His father clapped his hand down on his shoulder.

"You are no longer a child, and one day this will all belong to you. You might become Jarl one day, and you will be great, for those before you have done the same."

"Yes father," Alistair said. He pushed his mushed hair out of his face, and stared down at his feet.

"You were a surprise for this family, but a good one. Now, you must continue to practice with your sword, and till the land to grow your harvest. The gods will smile on you. Even now, Thor fights the giants on our behalf keeping us safe."

Thunder rolled in the background.

"We must prepare the party to head east, for I have heard of great booty there."

The door quickly opened, and therein rushed his older brother, Bjorn. His eyes wide with fear. "Father, we're under attack," he said.

"Alistair, take your brother and head to the hills."

"I will not leave your side," he squeaked. I could feel his fear, as he knees knocked.

"You must watch over your kin—your mother, your brother." His father rose, and rushed forward with his sword drawn.

"Remember, the gods will watch over you." The door slammed shut after Bjorn and his father.

"Mother, we must go to safety as father has said."

Instead, she reached down and cupped his cheek. "Love will not abandon." She handed him his sister. "You are to head to the caves with Evie, and not return until you receive the sign." She leaned forward and placed a chaste kiss on his forehead. "You are braver than you know, Alistair, my soft-hearted child."

She quickly picked up her shield and sword, then headed out the door where the sounds of the battle seeped through.

Alistair gathered his baby sister to him in the cloth swaddle, strapped a sword to his side, and inched out of the door towards the caves, to whence his mother had ordered him.

He raced away, leaving the sounds of the screams and metal hitting metal behind him, but he didn't get far. Upon turning a corner, he came face to face with the largest Viking he'd ever seen. His chest was bare, and black makeup covered his thick neck, and scarred face. He clenched a bloodied sword in his hand, and stalked forward.

Alistair looked around. No one could come to his aid. He'd never been tested.

"Are you the village idiot or only its weakling"?" the Viking asked.

Alistair remained quiet.

"You are the Jarl's son, and this place should belong to you since he is dead, just like your mother." He wiped the blood from his sword onto his pants leg. "So, let us make this easy for the both of us. Give me the baby so it can find its place on the rocks, and you my boy, will serve as my servant—a castrated one—then not even the weakest of women will want you."

I felt a heat bubbling within, as if scalding liquid had been poured over my hands and began to move upwards.

The Viking then ripped the baby from Alistair's arms and tossed it to the side. It cried out!

The heat grew all consuming. The rumble I thought was distant thunder was me. A deadly scream rose from Alistair's mouth, and he began to shift. His skin turned from its usual rosiness to that of an icy blue. Scales began to take shape, and within seconds, he transformed into a large dragon.

The Viking started to back up, sword still pointed upwards. "What in the name of Odin is this?"

"I've not been sent by Odin." Alistair's beast roared, and stepped forward. The earth shook beneath him.

The Viking raised his sword and struck, yet it did not pierce Alistair's thick dragon skin. It did nothing but anger him more.

With one terrifying roar, Alistair flapped his giant wings rising in the air, and released a stream of blue fire, burning the Viking down to his boots.

The sound of the baby's cries brought him back down to the ground. He could either save his village, and risk the life of his sibling, or abandon his sister in hopes of saving their father.

He took flight. Save the Jarl. Save his mother.

He flew overhead, burning those beneath him, but the bodies of his kin had already grown cold, just as the Viking had said. When he returned to get his sister, the baby was already gone.

He'd risked it all, and the gods had gifted him nothing.

I quickly kicked off the covers.

*Outside*. It was the one thing my mind kept shouting over and over, along with chanting I couldn't understand. I could feel a pull yanking me away from the safety of my room. I followed the tug if the unknown through the castle until I stood before a thick wooden door. I pulled it back and stepped across the threshold. The stars twinkled overhead, and I breathed in the fresh Highland air.

And there he stood. Alistair. His body glistened under the star's light. He moved without hesitation, thrusting his sword as if fighting an imaginary enemy—or only one that his memory made real. Each move was made with precision.

The closer I got, the more I could feel his rage which mirrored by own.

# Chapter 27

**LESLIE**

"I can't fight," I began. It seemed that as soon as someone turned into a supernatural creature they were supposed to have all of these amazing skills—magnificent lover, overachiever, and be able to leap buildings in one bound. "Lest we forget that up until a few days ago, I was a romance writer. My most active appendages were my fingers, and the most celebrated was my mind, along with all of the craziness that I could come up with.

"Yes, I am well aware of this. I don't know why I am to waste time teaching you a survivable skill, but the truth of the matter is men will come after you, and you will need to know how to protect yourself."

I didn't like that thought. My imagination ran wild and suddenly, this nice castle became a prison; the outside world would come barreling down the street with pitchforks, torches, and crowds marching because of their hatred for me, just like they'd done against Frankenstein's Monster.

"Oh my gosh, I'm Frankenstein's monster," I whispered.

Alistair began to chuckle. "Don't be ridiculous. I've lived here long enough to be able to vouch for your safety. However, that being said, things can change. Follow me."

He led me through the armory that housed tons of swords, automatic weapons that I couldn't identify, and even something that looked like a canon. "I didn't think we were about to fight the Jacobites again," I chuckled and pointed.

"Actually, we try to stay out of the political maneuvering of man."

He placed his hand on a digital keypad and pushed open a thick metal door. Therein, everything sparkled. It seemed more like a jewelry showcase room with everything in glass cases and recessed lighting, than an extension of the armory.

"Close your eyes, dear Leslie, hold out your hand and whisper, "Come to me."" I rolled my eyes at that and ground my teeth. Everyone deserved a chance to be trusted, but I didn't like that it had to start with me trusting him.

"I am your sire. I have no reason to do you harm, or I would have already done so."

"True, but for all I know, you are building a vampire army to take over the world."

"No dear, we are here to protect it."

I closed my eyes and did as he asked, and suddenly, something cool rested on my upturned palms. Cracking my eyes open, I stared in awe at the gleaming sword. Its blade was ornately carved with Viking Knot work and glowing runes. In its pommel rested a yellow jasper stone where a magnificent dragon was carved. I palmed the grip, and electricity raced up my arm, setting off my nerve endings.

The sword fit like a key and I was the lock. Holding it opened something within. It zinged me like I'd rubbed my feet too many times on carpet. I could hear my blood humming in my veins, whooshing as it flowed.

"Don't be afraid. Your sword dates back to the age of Boudicca, the warrior queen. It is connecting with you so that you will be the only one who can use her talents. You are the only one who can wield it."

From all that I knew, the Vikings had never made it to the Highlands, instead they'd remained pirates on the Scottish islands. What was a Viking dragon shifter, no less, doing in the center of the Highlands?

*Sweet*, I thought. Seemed like I was now going to become someone akin to the female Thor! Duh, duh, doon!

My vision blurred, and as if on fast-forward, blips of battle scenes formed in front of my eyes, where this sword gleamed and clanged. I watched as faceless warriors did flips and kicks, all while holding its magnificent grip. The dragon's image within the jeweled pommel sprung to life.

The images shifted, and the heartbeat grew louder.

It wasn't my own that I heard.

I shook my head to try and gain clarity.

"Leslie," it called to me.

"Leslie," Alistair shook my shoulder. "are you okay?"

"Sure, sure," I said twice. Once to reassure him and once to make it so I believed it myself.

THE IDEA THAT I WAS supposed to just instantly change into this mighty warrior made me feel as if I was submerged under twelve feet of water, drowning. My butt had been handed to me in more ways than one, as he laid me flat on the cave's floor.

In the deep dark cave, located beneath the castle, the dark walls were illuminated by lit torches. I stared upward at the stalactites, and listened to all the sounds around me—the bats further back, the water from the Loch's waves, and of course, the giant ass dragon waiting for me to get up, so he could knock me back down again.

It wasn't fair that he'd changed from this handsome man, with sharp pointy weapons, that I didn't know the name of without a google search, into this gigantic dragon that breathed blue fire.

What was I supposed to do with that? Carry around a fire extinguisher and hope for the best? I could still feel the hot flames singe my arm.

"*Too slow, Leslie*," he said. I didn't have to worry about him talking, he always seemed to find a way to speak right into my mind. Man, I missed when my mind belonged to me and the demons of creation that danced on my shoulders.

It was like fighting a dinosaur. His jaws snapped after me as I jumped and leapt off the cave's walls, dodged his thick tail, and tried to watch out for that fiery breath.

He didn't play fight. I'd had enough bruises to prove otherwise.

"I might heal fast, but that doesn't mean I don't get hurt," I pushed up and braced my feet to lean over and try to catch my breath.

"If you can fight me, and walk away, then you can fight anyone. Raise your sword."

My arm shook under its weight. He was in my head, and expected me to listen, obey. Maybe when he bit me, I'd given up any sense of freedom. Did his bite and blood mean that I had to serve him too?

"You know, diamonds are formed with pressure," he droned on.

"But if you keep this up, I'm going to die, just drop down a die."

He shifted back to his human form, and I tried not to watch him in all of his naked glory—buns of steel, and ripped abs that any model would envy. Broad shoulders and tall, just like I like them. Yummy.

I wasn't supposed to pay attention to him and his golden sun-kissed skin, though. That could only lead to more complications and even more problems that I didn't need. There could never be an "us."

My stomach rumbled.

"You need to feed." He said never turning to me. He pulled on jeans and a T-shirt, then padded over to the part of the cave that held essentials that others could so easily discover—yeah, a refrigerator filled with freshly produced animal blood, and their carcasses hanging on hooks. He got the meat and I the blood. Blech. Made my stomach turn.

"What does that mean, a nice table at the local eatery? I'd love a glass of Chianti." The local eatery would only have me looking at the other diners, though, and the Chianti, well, it just wasn't strong enough to get rid of that horrible taste of blood.

He headed to the refrigerator, opened the door and pulled out a bag of blood.

"Drink. I haven't had to do it this way in a long time, so I'm still under a learning curve." He handed me the package and I opened it. The putrid smell of fish mixed with a tang of iron.

"Fish?" I think I just threw up a little."

He grunted.

Could vampires starve? I mean, I'd do anything for a bison burger with blue cheese, and barbeque sauce, with double-fried fries.

"You must get used to drinking from animals. You are not allowed to drink from humans. Vampires are known to over-drink, especially newly made ones."

"Can't we try real food—like what I used to eat? And fish is not an animal, it's seafood."

He groaned. Today, it seemed that I was getting on his nerves, and this was not sexy at all.

"You're dead, Leslie. The blood is needed to keep you at least somewhat among the living."

This was hell, and that extremely gorgeous dragon there was the devil.

I squeezed my eyes shut, wrapped my lips around the plastic tube and tried to swallow the thick mixture down in one gulp. It stuck to the roof of my mouth and the back of my throat. I gagged, coughed, and tried to use my tongue to lodge it free. *Oh. This. Is. Hell.*

"Drink up. You still have six more to go." He chuckled. It was deep and charming, but I would have appreciated it more if it hadn't been at my own expense.

"You get to eat roasted goat, succulent and very well-seasoned I might add, and drink the best of wines, while I am allocated fish "juice"?"

He shrugged. I would have taken it all for punishment if I didn't think he knew any better. Sort of like the first-time dad who buys regular milk instead of formula.

"Oh, our reputations can't be that bad. I mean, what harm would it be to slip into town and check it out? I've not seen a lot of this place, and if I wish to return to my old life, I need to learn how to be around people."

"I've been meaning to talk to you about that," he began, and my stomach dropped. "You can't return to your old life"."

"Why the hell not? I live in the city that never sleeps and I guarantee they have a better supply of blood than this fish sauce."

He ran his fingers through his thick wavy hair and I saw again how gorgeous he was. I pushed against that emotion.

"Because you are now beholden to me."

He moved closer, and closed the space between us. "There have been many women who have wished to tie me down. And now, you have this great honor."

He had the nerve to smile, a perfect smile. In those eyes, the color of the Egyptian desert sands, I watched something play in them; a mix of longing, control, and a fleck of anger that was barely hiding under the surface. He wasn't any happier about this than I was. I guess his feelings didn't matter right now either. Before I had time to think about what I was doing, I struck out and smacked him.

"You knew this the entire time, and instead of letting me die, you brought me here to an existence that is nothing more than a horror show. I'm trapped and caged in this place, with some type of LARP play, and you're playing pretend, being heroic, but all that we have is this pretend and cursed reality.

If the gods have spoken to you, the only thing they've done is cursed you, and now you've done the same to me."

I pushed against his shoulders, and rushed by him.

"You will not leave these grounds," he roared.

"What are you going to do, kill me? Surely, you'd just bring me back."

# Chapter 28

**LESLIE**

Alistair carried me up the stairs and placed me in one of the plush dining room chairs like I was a beloved princess instead of the super pissed off vampire that I was.

I cleared my throat, and tried to find my dignity. "So, tell me about yourself," I said it so nonchalant, as though this was part of my plan.

He chuckled and plopped down beside me. His anger all but evaporated. "I'd rather hear about you."

There was something sexy about a man who could carry me; he wasn't even out of breath, and his skin was hot to the touch through his satiny cotton dress shirt.

"Oh no, I insist," I said.

So, closed and with my anger quelled, I could study him without question. Sure, I didn't know if I even liked him, but he so reminded me of my hero, Ian Macleod—just like he'd stepped right out of one of my books, but so much better. For a moment, I forgot myself and only wanted to lick his abs. That thought must have transmitted quite strongly.

"Licking abs?" he asked.

I'd never been one to blush, but I'm sure he felt my embarrassment. I looked away.

"Are there no secrets here?" I asked. Why did it feel like I was strolling through a thorn-filled nightmare? I leaned forward. "Are you a devil, a demon sent to torment me?"

He threw back his head and the laughter that erupted happened to ease the tension.

"I can't do this." He waved his hand and what at first was a table to seat twenty reduced to an intimate table for two. "Is this more to your liking?"

"You can't wield magic," I said.

"No, my dear, but you can." I looked down at my hands and saw them closed together, as if I'd clapped and made the table shrink.

He reached for my hand, and a snap of energy raced from me to him. The attraction, no matter how crazy, was there, but I knew I needed to keep my distance. He might be nice to look at, but that didn't mean he wasn't insane, that this wasn't insane.

Yet the flashing thought of buying expensive boutique lingerie sure did get the libido pumping. I'd come across so many decadent designs during my research, but right now, I'd be happy for him to throw me across the table and stake his claim.

My gaze rested on his lips.

I crossed and uncrossed my legs to get comfortable.

"Um, what's happening?"

"The mating ritual," he began, and placed his hand on my knee.

I pulled away. "You have to be a little more specific."

"By saving you, my soul was split, and through my blood, you were able to return to your body, and my blood powered your body's movements. Since your body is endued with that from me, it automatically seeks my touch and... connection."

I squinted. "Are you saying that since I'm your vampire, I'm now going to want to bone you all the time?"

"Bone?"

"Sex, sleep with, shag, have sexy time?" This was Gran's dream and my nightmare. I didn't do one-night stands, and the only emotional connection I had with him was anger, but that didn't stop me from imagining ripping his clothes off and finding out how strong our connection could be.

"Can't believe you want to talk about fur coats and knickers."

I couldn't roll my eyes hard enough. For all that he was, beast or not, he was still a man, a ridiculous, funny man.

I waited until the mirth died down. "What happens if we have sex? Strings, or no?"

I wasn't quite sure if I wanted to kill him or screw him. My hormones pushed to one extreme while my building rage the other. Both emotions sang louder and louder in my ear; each wishing to woo me to their side. Devil. Sexy devil. It was a wash.

"Our bond will get stronger from what I have learned from the reading, but I don't know as I've tried to avoid things of this nature at every cost."

Oh my gosh! He wasn't overjoyed about this either, and I thought it was just me. It must be terrible to have all of this pressure on your plate, and then be so alone.

I batted my eyelashes as I'd seen done in one of those old Elizabeth Taylor movies that Gran liked to watch and leaned forward, as if interested. "It must be so hard to be you, and so...alone."

Ding. Ding. Ding. We have a winner.

Surrounded by beings, he was still alone, unable to be connected with anyone, and so the equivalent of a deadly blind date persuaded him to save me. He put his desires on the line to save me from death, and to keep me with Gran. That was pretty honorable, right?

"I know you don't wish to be here, and although your ship is gone, I wish I could take you to town and get you back to your life."

"If you could, you'd do that? Even with the deadly costs of it all?"

He nodded. "I was raised to be honorable. What good would it be for you to remain here if you are to be unhappy? What good could come from your being here if you do not desire to be here, to be here with me, and as the seer of the Order? But alas, I cannot."

His question was too complicated.

Reason said that I needed to find a silver lining: *This is a once in a lifetime opportunity. You could have everything, all the information you need for your books right here, if you stay. But at what cost? In New York I barely had a dime to make ends meet, struggling with the ever rising cost, but here everything could be served on a silver platter.*

*The more I considered his options, the more I considered him as part of the equation.*

"Come, you have had a night worth forgetting," Alistair rose, but I stayed seated. "Let me show you back to your room, and tomorrow, you can decide as to what it is you'd like to do. But, surely, your life back in New York is missing you." When he realized I wasn't planning on going back to my room, he sat back down.

I wasn't ready to let those thoughts go, and be distracted by pretty words. Instead I stared down at my hands; hands that had ached for the art of craft through paper cuts, carpal tunnel, and too many carbs. The idea of returning to New York, especially with my tail between my legs, didn't appeal to me. I could almost hear the gossip at the local coffee shop—another mid-lister dropped. Until I found a way to break out, and bring my characters and world to life, they'd be right. I loved my readers, and I didn't want to let them down by not continuing the series either.

"Let's see how things are tomorrow. Maybe... maybe I can rearrange my plans. I was planning on working on a book—"

"Yes, set in the Highlands. I can be your personal guide," he seemed quite excited about that possibility. He practically glowed!

"And what of your wife?" I don't know why I threw that question out there, but men like him barely came unattached, and I didn't like forming bonds with unavailable men.

"Luckily, I am no one's mate, but yours. There is no outstanding girlfriend, fiancé or wife for you to worry about. Why, do you plan on filling that unoccupied position?"

Instead, I leaned back in my chair and wondered: What was there to lose for allowing myself to enjoy my time here?

"Do you have a phone I can use?"

A pleasant smile spread across his face that made my stomach do my little flip, as if butterfly wings fluttered and flapped. I stabbed some French fries with my fork, stuck it in my mouth and gagged.

I cleared my throat and tried to wash away the horrible taste with sweet wine. The French fries tasted like molded bread, the wine like vinegar. I frowned, dropping my fork, hearing the high-pitched clatter of silver as it landed on the china plate. I forced the awful crud down—*goodbye fresh hot fries; adieu dessert wines – and shuddered. Yuck!*

"Excuse me," I said. "That wasn't the reaction I was expecting from the food."

He frowned. "Since you were able to get down the fish, you should have been able to enjoy this lovely spread.

"This new vampire diet is going to have me eating fresh beef from the pasture."

"No, no, we'll figure it out." His eyes crinkled. Sort of like a beau would attend to his love interest.

I watched him. Why was he able to dance in my mind and watch me squirm? The small smile told me more than enough. He liked to be in control. That was his end game.

When I was younger, I used to skip rocks on the pond near my house in hopes of one day that those rocks would be worth a wish, a hope, a dream. Yet, as I sat there across from him, I felt torn between reason and what ifs.

Trying. I'd spent my entire life trying to make this work, pushing stones up a mountain to be crushed by it when it came crashing back down on me.

Yet, seeing him, my fantasy in real life, I wondered what I could lose besides my soul, my heart, my life, in believing that this could be more than I had ever wanted.

We'd been in this place before. This moment before.

"You've been alone so long, are you going to continue to push me away?" I asked him. It was his turn to take issue with my nearness. To watch him wonder as to my intentions.

"I can satiate your appetite and teach you all things to survive, but you must trust me," Alistair said and closed the distance between us""

Enough with the games.

To get a different outcome, I needed to do something different.

"What are the rules of magic here?"

"There is one main rule we must always follow: this supernatural world is to remain a secret. We are unable to share it with anyone. Listen, Leslie, you have many questions, but first, you must sleep. Accept this gift which I can give you, a gift of peace."

"I don't want peace. I want answers."

"Tomorrow the sun will reveal all, until then, you must understand that there is much you don't know and will learn soon enough. Not from the mouths of others, but from experience. When you rise tomorrow, your questions will be answered."

"And why can't you tell me now?"

Because dawn is on the horizon, and I must sleep. That is how the magic works here. By the moon's light I am free to come and go, but by dawn's early rays, back into the stones I must go."

He rose and paused at my seat. He went to walk by me, and I felt the slightest of shivers move through me, as if a puff of energy left his body to crash into my own.

How was this possible?

"Since you are my mate, what am I to call you?"

"What's in a name, my dear?"

"Everything. For the true name of the dragon has power to bring it to your feet."

He leaned in close and whispered it into my ear. His breath warm on my cheek. His skin smelled of fresh air. So close, I stared into those golden eyes and felt the magic and thrill of him being near.

"When you are ready, then we shall see where this is allowed to go."

Alistair stepped back, bowed his head, and disappeared from my sight.

"He's your eternity," Gran suddenly appeared at my side.

"Have you been waiting to pop out to come say something?"

"Well, I've been waiting to say something. I will never understand you, girl, or why you didn't let him swipe everything off of that table and show you what the gods made him with. Mmm."

"Gran! You grew up during a very repressed time. How is it that all you talk about is my shagging this guy"?"

"Didn't you just answer your own question? Plus, between all of the hot and heavy looks, I'm just happy that I didn't walk into a room smelling sperm. You know it must be hard to get out of a dining room table cloth, I'm guessing. I don't know how Dragon sperm is—if it would be more human than beast."

I stuck my fingers in my ear. The last thing I was even going to consider was my Gran's anatomy lesson on Alistair.

"He's all man, Gran."

I didn't know about love, but there was some interest there, and although I wasn't usually that type of girl, the longer I stared at him, the more I wondered if I could become her after all. The house, this man, the secrets, all offered and rolled out on a red carpet.

"Well, if that's the case, you've already ridden the dragon. Now, you need to find a way to ride that man. It is the cost of your survival, dear. It's time to screw the pooch, and I'm going to show you how!"

# Chapter 29

**ALISTAIR**

"I'm surprised you just let her walk away," Killian sat stirring the fire with a poker.

Alistair entered the library and barely closed the door before Killian began his talk. "Is this when you give me that brother-to-brother talk on how I'm to woo this woman?" Alistair asked.

"I didn't think you were a wooer?"

"I'm not, but I have to make sure that she fits here."

"That's the least of your concerns."

My job is to—"

"I'm going to stop you right there. If you don't find out who's attacked the woman in town and killed her, you are going to have a revolt on your hands. Everyone is pointing at the new vampire, and you don't want to see it."

"What are you suggesting?"

Killian cracked a smile, and pulled his leather coat further around him. "Well, she's going to need an alibi, and what better alibi than for her to be in your bed."

Alistair groaned.

"Hear me out."

"You've been dealing too much with the American Order to think that I'd just hop into a sexual relationship with her. That would be scandalous."

"Well, it will also be scandalous if the house rises up and decapitates you, but that is all on you if you so decide."

Alistair began to pace. "It will have to lead up to that. I'm not going to head to her room, knock on her door, and say, "Well, my dear, to keep you safe, let's shag."

"Even I wouldn't say it like that. You have to talk about her beauty, and try to heat up the oven before you try to roast the turkey."

Ever since they were young, Killian had always had his way with the females of the house and town. Maybe it was his bad boy aura, shaggy hair and that when he got upset, he'd bare his wolf-like canines. Women fell all over him with because of his brooding look, while for Alistair, no interest could be discerned until they learned of his status. Then, of course, everyone sought the high position at his side, but no one ever truly sought him out. Except Rose. He shuddered at the thought.

"I have a plan that will let you keep one head and get the other polished."

"Don't be so crass."

Killian chuckled. "You've been feeding her fish, and more than likely since you gave her your blood as the sea serpent, and not in your shifter form, , that is why she can only eat the fish of the sea."

Alistair groaned. He should have thought of that. In his haste to make things right, he'd taken what they had tons of: fish from the Loch, and given it to her. Now, that was all her body could digest.

"She must be starving?" Worry spiced his words.

"That is where you come in. She is now a pescatarian, and that means she can eat fruit of the sea. Take a platter upstairs to her, and seduce her. But you mustn't let her bite you, or drink from you again."

Alistair frowned. "If that is part of the vampiric ritual, what is the harm? "We are already tethered to one another."

"Should she drink from you again, that could create other issues that we don't know of."

"Such as?"

"She is the seer, able to absorb the traits of other supernaturals. What would it mean if through her bite, she also absorbed the part of you that made you a demigod?"

"So, I could face losing my immortality until I heal?"

"Yes, even more, she, in that state, would be virtually unstoppable."

"Do you know enough about her to even commence the greatest woo of your lifetime"?"

Alistair's gaze fell on the paperback.

"Yes, dear brother. I think I have a way in."

ALISTAIR CARRIED THE platter filled with freshly prepared sushi, along with the latest algae based cocktail, and her book. This was his one shot. He paused before her door.

He didn't want to consider that his being at her door had less to do with the thought of those under his care usurping his authority; nor did it have to be about any outside threat. There was one reason: Leslie.

He liked how her skin smelled like lavender, her eyes lit up with flecks of blue, like the most beautiful of sapphires, and that smile. He tried to catch himself. Dragons were loners. Until she arrived, he'd spent most of his time away from the castle, but now, he couldn't find the strength to swim away. She'd given him purpose to call this home again.

And that damn book.

*How could her Ivan really be me?*

He took a deep breath, adjusted his shirt, and tapped on the door.

"Come in," her voice was filled with light.

Light could show paths, reveal hidden treasures, and even the slightest glimmer could break through the expanse of darkness.

"I thought you might be hungry," he said and crossed the threshold.

He'd never expected to find her seated on her bed, legs crisscrossed in a pair of black and white polka dot, long-sleeved pajamas, with thick fuzzy socks, while wearing a turmeric yellow face mask,.

"Uh, I'm sorry I must be intruding."

Leslie jumped up. "Oh no, I couldn't sleep, and your pantry had enough of everything to make this mask. Turmeric can be so expensive, but I was happy to find it in your fully-stocked kitchen. Makes me want to do some YouTube videos, or maybe post an online review on the benefits of turmeric." She rambled.

"Since you weren't able to eat, I had the chef prepare something that might go down the hatch a little bit better. Do you like sushi?"

He placed the platter on the table near her bed where she stood.

"New clothes?"

"That nice maid dropped them off for me. She said that it would help me acclimate to life here if I had my own clothes. There is nothing like having fresh undies, and ones that I don't have to wash out every day, hang up over the shower rod, and...I'm doing it again. I tend to ramble when I get a little nervous."

"Am I making you nervous?"

He could see she weighed her options, deciding If truth would be his reward.

"Somewhat, but that has a lot to do with this change and new world. You've lived this life for much longer than I have. This is all new—up until recently none of this existed to me, and I didn't believe it ever could."

"I wanted to talk to you about that. I've been reading your book."

She smiled. "My book. You, a big brawny, manly man. You are enjoying my little paranormal romance?"

"Actually, yes. I think I can help you get your facts correct. You have a great grasp of dialogue, but your paranormal facets need to be straightened out a bit."

She began to laugh. "You do know all that came from my imagination."

"But it didn't."

"Whoa, I'm not a plagiarist."

"No dear. It would appear that as the seer, which you've always been, you've been able to tap into something that binds us. Your handsome hero, I fear is really me."

He heard the air whoosh from her lungs, her eyes grew the size of saucers, and her mouth began to gape.

"No, that... that can't be true. Ivan is not a dragon. "

Alistair took a step closer. "Would it be so bad for me to be your inspiration?"

"Take your shirt off. Take it off, now," she demanded.

"Uh, I think you're moving sort of fast to my getting naked."

"If you are the hero of my book—who just stepped off the pages—then I need to see for myself." He slowly began to open up his button-down shirt. "I feel like I need to do a dance with all of this."

"Don't make this even weirder." She moved closer to help him. His shirt slid off of his shoulders.

"Turn around. I need to see."

**LESLIE**

This was like being hit over the head with a hammer. I'd thought I'd created him from my mind, but no, it was from a shared memory.

I didn't care one bit about his naked chest.

The bittersweet truth smacked me in the face. I was even more of a failure than I thought, and it hurt.

My entire life, I'd had these stories inside me, and I thought it had to do with my discovering Gran."

"The gods have always looked down upon you."

"Bollocks, as you'd say. I'm not just an empty vessel to be filled with someone else's purpose, someone else's dreams. I have my own. I breath, I live, and now, you're taking that all away from me. I've only wanted this one thing, and just like that, you've erased it."

"Leslie, that is not why I am here."

"You came here only to be an ass to me. To take away the one thing that meant something to me. I fought tooth and nail to get my name on that cover—and it's not even my real name, instead I hid behind a name *they said* was more marketable. Something catchy. Something that people could remember, spell and generic enough to be on any shelf. All of the hours spent, and I could have just had you dictate it."

"I work eighty hours a week, alone, in the dark—eyes straining to type against the glaring white backdrop, with cramping hands, and it was all for nothing. It's not my story, but yours."

"But you're being foolish."

"Excuse me"?"

"You are. I've not taken anything from you. You've created my world and brought back memories I'd not taken time to remember in ages. It was almost like a poet's prayer, to almost hear my father's words again; to see my mother. Those are things that can't be so easily nullified."

"I don't know what to do."

"You are going to remain the fabulous woman you are, and realize that it is you who have made me the most fortunate of men, as not only have I been favored by your presence, but also with the knowledge that you indeed see me, understand me. And maybe one day, you could learn to love a simple, empty, broken man like me."

"I have nothing to offer you. I don't understand this world, and am not interested in knowing anything about it. I know the others don't like me, and aren't interested in getting to know me either."

"It is not you, love."

"Pray tell. What have I done to acquire their disdain? They don't have a problem with Gran. I'm sure she's going to find a way to the light at the end of this entire situation, like she'd walked in a church, prayed, and had a heavenly epiphany, while leaving me behind. And me? I'll still be stuck in between these two worlds."

"We can go and converse with my grandmother if that might help."

"What is she going to do? Tell me how to make fish soup."

He shook his head. "I'm sure the goddess Freyja would indeed get a chuckle out of that."

"As long as she can make it so that we can work this out, I might try it." Yet, the sight of sushi called my attention when my stomach rumbled again.

"But first, let's eat."

I plopped a piece into my mouth and waited for any sort of disgusting side effects. When nothing happened, it didn't feel so much like death after all. I'd eaten at some of the best sushi places in Manhattan; this was the creative fusion dish for the moment. At least it was better than blended fish parts, that was for sure.

"Oh, I don't think I can eat another bite." Food had never tasted so good. Spicy tuna, delicious wasabi. I stuffed my face, not even sure if I swallowed, to be honest.

"You are adorable."

"Ha! If that's your come-on line, then we really need to work on it."

He stared at me through starry eyes, and I had to ask, "If you find this turmeric mask attractive—"

"And what if I do? Have I abated any concern that you might have staying here?" He reached out and touched my face, then placed his thumb in his mouth. "I might just start liking turmeric after all."

"There you go, being charming again."

I didn't expect him to meet my challenge. I thought that would have been a natural barrier. He pulled me in.

"Hold that thought," I said and jumped up. If I was going to be kissed by this man, then we weren't going to worry about a yogurt and turmeric mask. I stumbled to the bathroom and scrubbed it off of my face—giving me a great natural glow.

"You can do this, Les"." My Lamaze breathing was back with chipmunk cheeks, as well as the inchworms that crawled in my stomach. A wave of nausea hit me mixed with anxiety.

Gran popped into the bathroom. "You know he's there waiting for you."

"Yes," I know."

"Then fix yourself up. Pluck, shave, spray—freshen up, dear. You don't want him to be turned off by your unkempt forest."

"Gran! Are we having this conversation"?"

"You've changed in front of me before, and I know that look hasn't been around for a few decades now. No one likes pubes. Of course, back in my day, the men were so happy just to get some, they didn't mind like these men today. I was thinking since I'm doing a little bit of flashing from corporal to incorporeal, that maybe I can find a way to get myself updated too."

"What do you mean?"

"Oh, the black is so gloomy. I don't feel gloomy here, but I do have tons of questions." A cigarette appeared out of thin air again in her long, thin cigarette holder. "But, we can talk about all of that after you boink him."

"Gran, you can be insufferable at times."

"Don't go getting upset with me. That's not going to do anything with making your libido go zippity, zappity, zoop. I'm trying to make things better. You've been tossed and turned so much in life, and he could be so good for you, if you'd only let him."

"Good or not, you are not to be in that room to assess his technique."

"Not even a peek? He won't know."

"No."

"Okay, okay. I'll behave and explore more of the castle."

I freshened up as quickly as I could and scrubbed until bubbles practically floated around the bathroom from all of the luscious suds.

Finally ready, I wrapped my towel around me, and opened the door only to be greeted by a handsome man asleep on my bed. Crappity, crap-tastic!

# Chapter 30

**ALISTAIR**

Awakening, he shifted in the bed, cracked open his eyes and remembered he hadn't made his way back to his chamber last night. Instead, cuddled up to his side, with her wild hair sticking up in every direction, her mouth slightly open, and an unladylike snore escaping her beautiful full lips, he tried not to laugh.

Although he would have enjoyed staring at her all morning, easing into the day with whatever this could become, duty called. He eased up from the bed, and was greeted by Gillianbusti. "What is it this evening?"

"There you are," Rose called out. "We were concerned about you, as you weren't in your usual hidey holes. As you know you need to get on board with our plan, show everyone a united force, especially since more details of the murder have been recovered."

"You're telling me this instead of taking me to the scene—again?"

"We couldn't find you, but I did bring you pictures. Hell, Alistair, even my wards only last so long. I still had to release the scene over to the police."

"What do you know about this one?"

He held her smart phone and flipped through the images. It could have been the same scene if it hadn't been a different body—a sigil, a drained and naked female with Leslie's book.

"Was she a reader?"

"Yes, but this crime had a stronger message."

"Show me."

Rose flipped a couple more images and handed him back the phone. "This wine glass."

"So, the killer had wine"?"

"No, the glass was filled with the victim's blood and enjoyed afterward. Fingerprints were left behind, and we've run them through the database. They came back as Leslie's."

Alistair shook his head. "That's impossible. She was with me all night."

"You sleep like the dead. She could have snuck out, then returned, and you never would have known."

"No, I know she didn't do it."

"You're going to have to face the honest truth. Your mewler is indeed killing people, and I'm going to have to take her with me."

"No!" He stepped in front of Rose, blocking her way.

"You are interfering with official business. I can only do my job and help you, if you allow me to."

"She can't even transform, she doesn't know how."

"So, since there is only one way out of that room, and if she can't sneak out as a bat, she should still be there"?"

"Of course."

Rose pushed past him and opened up the door to Leslie's room finding it empty. "So, where is your sweet vampire now?"

# Chapter 31

**LESLIE**

"You should be very happy that I got you out of there when I did," Gran began as she led me down a secret passageway that meandered through the castle. We walked through the dark and cramped hallways.

Gran passed me a sword she must have pulled off the wall. It was heavy as heck. I hoped I wouldn't need it, or accidently impale myself with the sharp blade.

I could hear the raised voices on the other side of the walls. Whatever had happened was serious, and it seemed to be the consensus that I was the one responsible for it.

"Where are you taking me?"

"To see what is really going on. They are saying that you're the one behind it all, but I know the truth. Come. We have to hurry, if we are going to save the next girl."

"The next girl?"

"Yes, she's being held at one of the tenant cottages."

"Why not get help"?"

"They aren't going to listen to me or you, as they're convinced you're behind it all. No, we have to save her before she dies."

The secret passageway led out into the garden, and under the cover of night, I followed Gran's shimmer. We stuck to the trees and shadows as not to attract any attention. Armed guards kept calling out my name like I was some kind of lost puppy. I could even feel Alistair mentally reaching out. How was it possible that he could think that of me too?

I pushed through the disappointment and hurt and glanced around. While still only in my socks, I raced in the direction Gran sent me to find the tenant's house all lit up.

"Hurry, she's dying"." Gran waved me forward, and then stopped. "But I can't go in. Should I? That sigil will also pull me under and through to the other side."

"I have no intentions of leaving. But whatever you do, you mustn't drink from her. That will be your death sentence and there is no way of coming back from that."

Grans voice was rarely stern, but this time, it was filled with righteousness, determination, and a sense of warning. The voice a mother used before she placed her child into time out. The full-bodied voice of warning that only Mom's around the world could share that overcame every culture and language. Her words were spoken in the language of Mom. I understood it.

"I'll take care of her, Gran," I said and burst through the door, to the most horrific scene ever. The young woman lay sprawled out, fully nude, and the gurgling sounds that came from the back of her throat as she tried to breathe, mixed with her panic and fear.

"It's going to be okay," I said, and felt my teeth descend. Blood. All of this fresh blood going to waste. The intoxicating smell lured me ever closer, until I stepped into the pooling crimson.

I'd never wished for the power to heal like I did then. "Gran, go get help."

"But if I leave you, you'll take a sip. All they need to see is if your taking one sip and then, poof, you're gone."

"You have to trust me to be stronger than that. I'm still in here; the same determined Leslie."

Gran paused only for a second, before she flashed away. "At least someone is getting a hold on their new situation."

I took the dying woman's hands, and the scene unfolded before me:

*While sitting on her couch, she casually watched the latest episode on BBC. The loud television muffled the sound of the slight knock at her door, until the slight knock changed into a loud bang.*

*She jumped, knocking over her glass of wine and popcorn. "Just great. I'm coming, but I don't see why anyone needs to stop by at this time of night."*

*She padded to the front and opened the door. Instead of a face, I only saw a blur. The magical face swam before me, leaving only a void.*

*"Good evening, may I help you?"*

*He didn't speak, but I saw in his leather-covered hands that he was indeed prepared.*

*"It is with great joy that I bring you your salvation, a sacrifice to the ultimate of gods." He said, and began to squeeze her neck.*

*The woman struck back, attempting to fight him off.*

I looked away. I didn't want to see anymore.

She urged me to look further.

*Once he had her under control, where she stopped fighting, he tossed a coin onto the floor, creating the purple sigil.*

*"Death of dawn, lightness of day, accept this offering, I pray," he said, and pushed her down onto the floor.*

*"Sorry for the mess," he said lastly, and began his procedure, only to hear the floorboard creek. The woman turned and there stood Gran at the door in her corporeal body, before she flickered away.*

That's how Gran knew. She's been exploring and stumbled on this.

And that also meant that he was still in the house waiting to finish it all up. I pressed down on the wound, applying as much pressure as I could, and with all the energy I had I reached out, hoping that the link I had with Alistair was indeed two-way.

I felt her last gasp, and saw from the corner of my eye as the man dashed out of the door towards the woods.

I gave chase.

# Chapter 32

**LESLIE**

Through the woods, over the hills, I followed the figure until I stared out into the expanse of empty wilderness—rugged Scottish mountains with large trees, babbling creeks, and talkative wildlife waited for me to near.

With the castle in the distance, away from the winding roads and life of Inverness, my hand gripped the sword's grip and I tried to breathe. Even under the cover of night, with only a sliver of the moon casting its light, I could make out in the inky shadows, but this was different. I could feel more than one pair of eyes staring back at me. One friend, and one quite maleficent.

A wolf's howl reached my ears and I saw him come bounding my way. His snarl loud and threatening.

I backed up.

Magic sifted through the Highland air falling onto my skin.

Just as the wolf was about to reach me, I struggled to hold my weapon and it leapt over me to fall on that which I'd not seen approaching.

The faint smell of freshly shed blood, combined with a very human scream, caused my hackles to rise. My canine's descended, a thirst beckoned me.

That aroma was like what fresh baked bread used to mean to me. I breathed through my mouth cutting off the aroma's appeal. The tanginess that was surely a trap.

With my sword raised, I inched toward the darkness, watching for the slightest movement.

My heart reacted to the tension, pulled tighter than a guitar string ready to be plucked.

I turned left first, then right.

"You really shouldn't go running off on your own," Killian said. He still had blood smeared across his mouth.

"Step back. I don't want to hurt you."

"Hurt me?" he frowned. "And why would you do that?"

I looked behind me to see if anything was there. "You're the one killing these women, and draining them dry."

"I assure you that I like my women very much living, well mostly alive. There is no fun in a cold body, and it's a waste of life for such beauty to be erased."

He took a step closer.

"Why are you out here then?"

"Why are you out here"?" he countered. "I am out for my nightly walk, and happened to stumble upon you, a mewler with a sword drawn. Are we looking for things that go bump in the night?"

Just then, a twig snapped, but it was too late. I watched a metal blade slide from Killian's back through his stomach. He howled in pain.

I dropped the sword and stumbled backwards as Lloyd approached.

"It is so good to finally meet you," he said. "and now I know why his Lordship has neither time nor interest in the things that are necessary and good."

I would have liked to have said that I saw the crazy but he wasn't a supernatural, but a man with a gun that could still kill a vampire like me.

"Come get going. I have a lot that I need to do with you, and daylight will be here soon enough."

He turned me around and put the muzzle of the gun into my back. "Don't try any funny moves either. You might be fast, but I'm sure these silver bullets are faster."

WE WALKED AND WALKED until I became disoriented, and then followed a narrow path to the mouth of a cave that overlooked the water. Once inside, he removed his flashlight and forced me further into the cave. The cave gave way to a makeshift lab.

Looking around, it would have appeared just like any other fisherman's retreat, well, if you took away the women he had caged up, suspended in the air with tubes leading from their bodies into various tanks. The clear tubing was stained red in color.

I finally understood. This is where he drained them.

He pushed me towards a waiting gurney, and tied me down.

Man, I really wish I'd spent more time practicing with Alistair, but how was I to know that he had a lunatic working for him?

The sound of titanium cuffs snapping down around my wrists and ankles signaled the beginning of the end. Whatever he had planned, I was a part of that.

"What are you planning on doing to me?"

"Making you into what you should be. Vampires were not created to be pescatarians. You are supposed to be a force to be reckoned with, not this little weak thing. No, what you need is what I can provide you with, and you will provide me something in return."

He placed a gas mask over his face, and then began to burn an herb I was familiar with: henbane. The smoke wafted, and my consciousness drifted.

WHEN I AWOKE, I FELT a tube in my mouth force-feeding me what tasted like bliss—human blood. It ran across my tongue and warmed me from within. Power mixed with zeal, and a thirst for more. I continued to drink until I was sure I'd had my fill.

"That should be enough." He then inserted an IV into my arm, attempting to draw blood from me.

Barely a drop came out.

"You know, you taught me this ritual years ago in your book. When I heard that you were the new one in the castle, I knew this would be something to make you happy. You could walk in your gods given destiny, and I could be your servant. I only need your blood to mingle with mine.

I drifted in and out of consciousness, and it seemed that I was almost floating.

*Alistair*, I called.

Lloyd removed the feeding tube. "Just imagine what I will be able to do once I am a vampire like you. I can finally take down that Nessie who eludes me, bring jobs back to the town, and make this place a national monument to increase tourism. I can save this town from what his Lordship can't see.

He created a tourniquet, pumped his fist, and withdrew his blood, then mixed it with my a drop of my own.

"Now, you only have to say those words. I can drink the blood and it will be all good and done."

I rocked my head back and forth. "That's only fiction. I don't know what you're talking about. I'm just a romance writer."

I tried to scrutinize the room, to find something I could use as a weapon.

"The bloody hell you are. You've written about this place, these people in your series—all of them, and just made them all appear. When you arrived, I knew it to be true. This was to be my way to make it all better."

I struggled against my metal cuffs. Clang. Clack. "Help," I screamed.

"No one can hear you back here. You will remain here with me until we get this done. No matter how long it takes, or what it means in the end. My town is more important than you."

I glanced over to the women in the cages. "How many do you have up there?" Each one of them had family, friends, a history, and instead of living life, they were dealing with a mad man in a cave who believed that he could be turned into a vampire.

"Waiting to be transformed? Hmm, maybe around nine. You know, nine is the holy number for us."

*I'm on my way.*

I just needed to buy time.

"How long have you been doing this? With these women?"

"It's not that simple, and these women, well, it's not like they have roots. They can be easily replaced in life. They are commodities, just like the cows and sheep that litter the fields. Vampires need a source of food—human blood—and that is what they shall be until they are emptied."

"Is that what happened to Bridget?"

"Oh, heavens no. I needed a way to get your attention. She reminded me of your character, Scarlet. You know, the one that is just horrible to everyone, and I thought she'd do perfectly as my sacrifice to you."

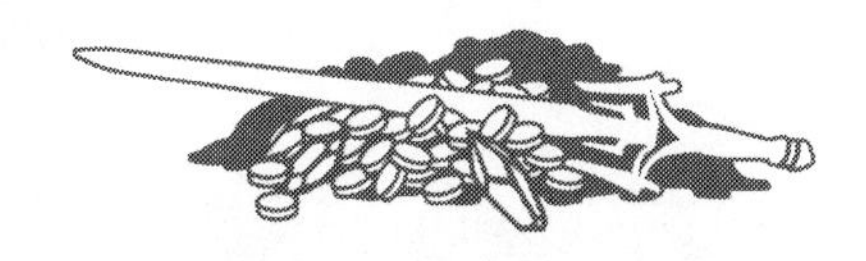

"YOU ARE THE MOST OBNOXIOUS man. I'm telling you that something bad has happened and you refuse to act," Gran screamed at Alistair, breaking her usual genteel and calm demeanor.

"I have no need to listen to anything you say, as you and Leslie have constantly disobeyed the rules of this house. Instead of following them, now you wish to lie and tell me of a human woman being killed on my property, which Leslie just happened to stumble upon."

"Gran swirled around him, winding like a tornado. "No, she was in her room, and I went to get help, as I thought Leslie was the only one who'd be willing to help, and I was correct. Instead of assisting this poor woman, you've done the most cowardly of things—nothing. Anyone can do nothing, that does not make you an adequate ruler, that makes you one filled with privilege. Nothing you have done since we've been here has been for anyone other than yourself. You sir, are a bastard and a selfish one at that."

"Alistair," Killian limped into the throne room.

"Killian what has happened?"

"Leslie's been taken," he painfully whispered.

"I've been trying to tell him about the girl down on the property, the one bleeding out with Leslie," Gran said.

"No, it's gotten worse then. She must have given chase. While I was out for my nightly snack, she was overpowered. I tried to help her as much as I could."

"Head over to see Peter and have him treat your wounds. You'll recover. I will go—alone—in search of Leslie. They can't be far, and I will attend to this matter without help."

"You foolish, foolish man," Gran grumbled. "You might make everyone else bow to your foolishness, but nothing will stop me from searching under every rock, in every cave, and behind every tree to find her. If you will not be man enough to be her hero, then you are not worthy of her. Now, get out of my way. My granddaughter needs me."

Gran disappeared, and Killian stood there, holding his side.

"She's right, you know. You've been filled with this illogical pride and prejudice of who you believe Leslie is supposed to be, that you are now unwilling to help. That woman has done nothing but try to help you to retain your leadership position, but you've fought her at every turn. You've demeaned her, and not treated her justly. Dear brother, if this was a romance novel, I dare say, you'd not be the hero after all.

Killian limped away, and still Alistair sat. He closed his eyes and reached out with his mind, searching for her. His mind's clouded image took shape and the shadows revealed her location.

What good was a connection if he couldn't find her without even moving?

He scanned the area, reaching for her essence.

With her destination in mind, he raced down to the depths of the castle, tossed off his clothes and dove into the water. Cold waves washed over him, and the deeper he dove, the more his body stretched, twisted and turned.

*Hold on love, I'm coming!*

The air hummed with his arrival. And his loud screech shook the cave walls.

Lloyd clapped. "What a wonderful day! Nessie has arrived too. Who would have thought it possible"?" He moved towards a stainless-steel cabinet and opened it up, therein rested enough weapons for an army to fight—automatic and semiautomatic weapons, along with grenades. He retrieved his harpoon and moved back towards the cave's entrance.

If I didn't get up, the ass would die, and I'd feel guilty about it. And since he saved me from true death, I had to try to do the same.

Focusing all of my energy and strength on the stainless steel cuffs, they began to stretch enough for me to pull my hands free.

I quickly ripped them off of my feet, and grabbed one of the guns he'd left behind. Thank the gods for the citizens police academy; at least I knew how to use an automatic rifle. I loaded it, and rushed after Lloyd. Alistair, even with his dragon's breath, might not be too much of a challenge against a sharp, modern-day harpoon.

It might end up being emasculating, but at least he'd be alive.

I moved forward and took aim. "Halt," I yelled. "Don't make me shoot you, Lloyd."

"I can't let Nessie slip away this time."

"If you shoot that creature, I'm going to shoot you."

"But I have your blood." He held up the beaker, tilted his head back and drank it.

To me, it reminded me of those people that liked to fry pigs' blood, or include the steak juices from the package into the pan.

He swallowed it and my face twisted in disgust. It dripped down his chin from the corners of his mouth, and he wiped it away with the back of his hand. I waited for the true reaction—nausea, regurgitation, and possible death. It was like drinking a mixture from a corpse, and that's exactly what I was. I mean, would you take a straw to the funeral home and take a sip? Just yuck!

Alistair closed in, ready to blow fire, and as Lloyd took aim, so did I.

My vision allowed me to see every nuance of his motion, and before he could pull the trigger on the grenade harpoon, I fired off two rounds.

Crap. I missed,

And so, I fired two more.

I hit my target, and Lloyd screamed out in pain. The harpoon dropped from his hands, firing and striking Alistair square in the chest, only to bounce right off.

Guess he didn't need my help after all.

And maybe I didn't really need his, or him.

# Chapter 33

**LESLIE**

When Rose entered the cave with her paranormal investigative team, I tried to be civil. She'd accused me of being the evil in their midst, not even wanting to look at the other suspects. She must have been a jealous woman to just want to alleviate a threat, even if that threat had nothing to do with the actual crime. There might have still been feelings between Alistair and Rose for all I knew, but their dysfunction wasn't what I'd wanted, needed, or even desired to be around.

And with Alistair, I didn't want to talk to him, let alone share a roof with him. This debacle was a palate cleanser. I could look at Alistair and see the potential in him, but I didn't need a man that required fixing. There were too many issues of my own which now needed tending to.

Alistair walked over in full human mode; his dragon long gone. "So, is this where you tell me goodbye?"

"I hadn't planned on telling you anything. Somehow or another you still have a lot of growing up to do. How you can be centuries old and not know how to treat a woman is beyond me. I don't have time for a fixer-upper project."

"A project, is that what I am?"

I considered my words carefully. "You said that pressure makes diamonds, well, maybe you too need to be shined up a bit. I can't give up my life for you. After a while, I'd end up hating you more than I already do for what you took from me. You gave me life, but you can't just take away the life that I've been building for myself."

Alistair glanced down at his feet. "You're right, Leslie. I didn't treat you very well, and that had to do with me, not you."

I nodded. "That doesn't change anything. You could learn a lot from Killian. In fact, you should take a few lessons from Killian on how not to be a giant asshole." I brushed passed him, thinking that at one time I believed we could have been something.

Yet, I heard the vampire within still say, "*Mine.*"

"Leslie!" Gran raced into the cave, giving everyone the stink eye. "Are you okay?" I could see her panic, and when she wrapped her arms around me, now that was home. I'd never been so relieved to fall into her arms. Tears began to well.

"Don't you let them see you cry. They'll take it for weakness, but you sure did have this old woman worried. I liked it better when I was just a ghost. I know I asked you to stay here, but I really think we were better off in Manhattan."

The sun began its rise, and soon the castle, those nocturnal like me, would feel the need to sleep.

"Well, I did have enough of an adventure to start that next book," I said. "

Gran shook her head. "I'll never understand where all of these characters come from."

"Me either, but I'm sure the ideas are there."

Slathered down in sun block, and covered with long sleeve clothes and a large hat, letting almost no sun peek through, I pulled on my sunglasses and cast one last look at the castle. There was no sadness, just indifference. Nothing had given me reason to stay, and everything had forced me to go.

Once away from the enchanted castle and land, Gran returned to her ghostly form, and we both heaved a sigh of relief. I couldn't escape that place fast enough—credit card balances and all be damned.

I caught the first plane back to New York, and with the press getting the news of my arrival, it seemed that it was good to return from the *dead.* The paparazzi swirled with their lights and cameras until I had to get security to catch a taxi home.

Claudine stood outside my door clutching newspapers to her side, as well as a large coffee.

"It's the afternoon," I said. "and I'm dead tired."

"Well, you're going to need to fix your face soon. Looks like the big guys have taken notice of your recent numbers. I've been able to schedule you for tomorrow morning's news shows.

" Donovan was arrested and is awaiting his first court hearing, especially since you returned. I'm guessing the DA wants to make sure to get his case closed, and quickly."

"It took long enough."

"Sorry, that's my fault." She blushed. "Anger got the best of me." That was putting it nicely. They'd both been escorted off of the ship, and taken to the magistrate for it all to be sorted out.

"If you weren't my sister, I'd so fire you."

"Got to get it in when you can"." She shrugged, then continued. "And Maurice called. He said that he's taken a fresh look at your proposal and thinks he can sell it now."

I gritted my teeth, and stretched out my hand again. "Taxi!"

"Where are you going?" Claudine asked.

"To take care of some final business."

Wearing my still-wrinkled clothes from my too long of a flight, I bypassed security with a smile. I then caught the elevator up to the eleventh floor where Maurice's private office was located—not where he'd meet clients.

The elevator doors slid open, and I pasted on the most perfect of smiles. Something had changed within me.

"Ma'am," you can't go back there," said the receptionist.

"But I can, and you're going to buzz me in."

"Sure," the receptionist said, and the glass door unlocked.

With his corner office, Maurice was supposed to be one of the best in the business. His view overlooked Central Park, a view that most would envy. Even with his expertise, he hadn't performed. And it was time to cut those from my life who suffered from underperformance.

"Maurice," I said, then stepped across the threshold into his office.

"Leslie, oh my, it's good to see you. I'd heard you were lost at sea. What a miraculous return. I've been fielding so many calls for you. The press is loving your reappearance, as are your fans. I can't wait to see what we'll be able to make possible with your career now."

I took a seat, leaned back into the chair, crossed my legs and stared at him in silence... until an uncomfortable silence built up between us. He tugged at his collar.

He cleared his throat. The confidence in his voice evaporated like hot air. "I think I owe you an apology."

"Oh no, what you owe me is my letter reverting my publishing rights back to me."

"That's not possible, Leslie."

"But it is. You fired me, and with, me goes my work."

"Please, Leslie, you can't do that. In the last couple of days, you've sold more books than any other author over the history of us taking numbers. We can't keep up with the demand."

"I guess that's something you should have considered before you were so callous. Now, take out that paper and get to typing. I can wait."

I waited patiently for my letter, where all of my books and ownership would be reverted back to me.

"You're ruining my life." He reached in his desk and pulled out a paper bag and began to blow in and out.

"Oh, but I'm sure your life can change too with a horrible cruise. Even more, with the publisher losing so much money, there is no telling what sort of cruise it might be. Anyway, I hate to just demand and dash, but I have a couple of interviews to get to."

I held on tightly to that letter. Never again would anyone walk all over me. That was the great things about now being a vampire—that confidence.

I might still have a lot to learn, and there would be a great learning curve too, but at least I wouldn't have to stop being Leslie Love to do it.

"Ms. Love?" The receptionist called after me. "You forgot your check."

I smiled. Enough numbers to start all over.

Who knew that once bitten, I'd get exactly what I wanted? To be me.

# Epilogue

**LESLIE**

I'd found a way to keep my hunger at bay. Nothing like sushi for that, and back in our apartment, Gran and I reverted to our usual routine.

It felt good to be home.

"Have you heard anything from him"?" Gran asked.

She didn't need to name him; we both knew who she meant: Alistair. Even thousands of miles away, something inside of me still called out to him—every night, every second of every day—as if a part of me was missing.

I squashed that, though, by stuffing myself with more sushi, and working on the next Ivan Macleod book. With all of that historical fodder, I had to do something with it.

I shook my head.

"You know though, dear, I've been thinking about something, something that isn't quite clear. Lloyd was using magic, right?"

"Yes," I said, still punching the keys to accomplish my daily word count.

"Magic, really? There's just something that is bothering me here with what he did." Besides the whole serial killer thing?"

"Well, not a serial killer, but more of a spree killer." She ignored me and continued to talk.

"There are rules to magic, a system even. It is not just used willy-nilly."

I paused. When I was there in that cave, I'd thought of the same thing. For someone who was interested in the occult and its practices, he sure wasn't well versed in all of it.

"Was he born of magic? Blessed by the gods, or did someone give him something that might make him more magical"?"

"So, how did he cast the spells?" Gran asked.

"The sigils." I stopped typing, lost in thought.

If he wasn't magical, how did he cast the spells?" Gran stepped in front of me, concern marring her face.

We stared at each other.

Lloyd might have been involved, but he wasn't the top of the maleficence there, like what I'd felt in the forest. There was something else, someone else, and they were indeed powerful if they wished to attack a community filled with supernatural beings. As the seer, I would soon be called on to fight a battle I wasn't sure I could win. After all, I was just a romance writer who loved hot men in kilts, Vikings, and maybe even dragons. But even more, as a vampire connected to Alistair, I knew I had to help. He could not go this alone. I wouldn't let him. "Oh my god. Oh my goddess," I started to hyperventilate.

"Calm down. It's not like we know anything. It's all just speculation." Gran pulled another cigarette from thin air and began to pace.

"That means that they are still in trouble. The entire village. The entire castle"." Numerous faces drifted through my mind.

And that's when my phone rang.

I picked it up on the second ring. "Leslie, this is Killian. I hate to bother you, but this is about Alistair."

"Oh no, what's happened"?"

"He's disappeared." I'd have to be stronger than I ever thought I could be, and save the man I was tied to for the good of us all, or go down trying.

"I'll go start the packing," Gran said, and put her cigarette out.

"This time we're flying."

The End

Find other fabulous stories about Tina Glasneck, and learn more about her dragons in The Dragons series.

www.TinaGlasneck.com[1]

Newsletter

www.TinaGlasneck.com[2]

1. http://www.tinaglasneck.com/

2. http://www.tinaglasneck.com/

# About the Author

TINA GLASNECK ENJOYS creating stories that combine history, mythology, Norse Gods, and dragons. Someday she might just fancy a trip to Asgard too, and find out what all the fuss is about! Read More from Tina Glasneck at: www.Tina-Glasneck.com[3]

3. http://www.TinaGlasneck.com

89602826R00112

Made in the USA
Columbia, SC
17 February 2018